The
Incompetent
Cat

AND

Other Animal Tails

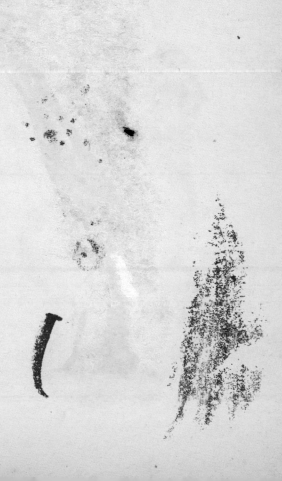

The Incompetent Cat

AND

Other Animal Tails

Edited by
Grace Fox Anderson

Illustrated by
Janice Skivington Wood

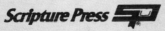

Scripture Press

Amersham-on-the-Hill, Bucks, HP6 6JQ, England

ISBN 1 872059 29 5

Scripture quotations are from
the *Holy Bible, New International Version* (NIV),
© 1973, 1978, 1984, International Bible Society.
Published by Hodder & Stoughton.

'Sly Thief,' 'An Arctic Bear,' and 'Bashful Runner,' were originally published
in *Story Friends* by The Mennonite Publishing House. 'Brian and the Blind
Cockerel,' 'The Fox Watch,' 'The Trouble with George,' 'The Incompetent
Cat,' and 'The Runaway Cow' (previously 'What Happened to Thirteen?')
were previously published in *Discovery* by Light and Life Press. 'The Return
of Midnight' was previously published in *Youth's Story Paper* by The
American Sunday School Union. 'Deadly Eddie,' 'The Windup Dog,' 'Mule
Sense,' 'The Camel,' 'Look, Mum—No Hands!,' 'The Secret of Tawachi
Mountain,' 'Casey, the Crow,' 'A Horse Named "Robert Raikes",' 'Wolf!,'
'How to Wake Up a Dormouse,' 'The Christmas Trap,' 'The Intruder,' 'The
Suitcase Bird,' 'My Friends, the Wrens,' 'The Day of the Dust Storm,' and
'Where Is Snow?' were all previously published in *Counselor* by Scripture
Press Publications, Inc.

Production and Printing in England for
SCRIPTURE PRESS FOUNDATION (UK) LTD
Raans Road, Amersham-on-the-Hill, Bucks, HP6 6JQ by
Nuprint Ltd, 30b Station Road, Harpenden, Herts AL5 4SE.

Contents

The Incompetent Cat

A Fiction Story by Gay Seltzer

NO ONE KNEW exactly what age Monster the cat was. In fact, no one was absolutely sure when Monster first decided to become a member of the McDonald family.

'It was in the summer,' Terry said. 'Don't you remember? He climbed the apple tree and tried to bat the apples down? Only he got stuck on a branch, and Father had to climb up and get him!'

'You're wrong,' said Tony, Terry's twin. 'He came just before winter. Remember the first time he saw snow? He thought it was sand and began to roll in it—and looked like an ice lolly! We had to wrap him in towels.'

Father looked at the sleeping cat, one paw curled around his eyes. 'Why does he have to sleep right under my feet?' he asked. 'I must have stepped on him a hundred times.'

'Because he's a monster,' Mother said, and everyone laughed.

They had all agreed on his name. The thin, bedraggled cat had appeared one morning at breakfast-time. As Terry opened the door to let him in, the dirty grey cat spied his

reflection in the hall mirror. Hissing and spitting, the ball of fur jumped on the kitchen table, knocking over a pint of milk. He raced across the table and leaped to the floor, leaving milky footprints everywhere he went.

'What's the matter with that cat?' Mother had screamed.

Terry was the first to pick up the shaking grey creature. 'He's just scared, Mum. He thought his reflection was a monster.'

'I rather think he is a monster,' Mother had said.

So 'cat' became Monster, and Monster had stayed.

Terry and Tony stretched out on the rug in front of the fire. Monster opened one eye and moved closer to the flames.

Mother shook her head. 'Boys, move that ridiculous cat,' she said. 'His tail is almost in the fireplace.'

Terry scooped him up. 'Monster, you're worse than a baby. Can't you learn anything?'

Monster purred and went back to sleep.

That night everyone was awakened by shrieking and yowling. Mother turned on the landing light, and Terry and Tony followed Father downstairs to see what was causing the rumpus. As Father turned on the kitchen light, everyone could see Monster jumping up and down in the corner. His back was arched and the hair on his tail stood straight up.

'What's going on here?' Father yelled.

Terry bent down and looked under the table while Tony picked up the trembling cat.

'I think he's just scared,' Terry said. 'There's a grasshopper under the table.'

'A grasshopper!' Mother cried. 'Cats are supposed to catch grasshoppers—not go into a panic!'

'I don't think Monster knows that, Mum,' Tony said.

'That worthless cat,' Father muttered. 'I don't even think Monster knows he's a cat.'

Terry picked up the grasshopper and threw it out of the back door. Mother shook her head and followed Father back up the stairs.

'Turn out the lights, boys,' she said, groaning. 'And do something with that cat.'

At breakfast the next morning, Father made an announcement between yawns. 'From now on, Monster sleeps outside. No arguments. That's final.'

That night after dinner, as the flames died down in the fireplace, Tony and Terry looked up at Father. Father looked back, yawned, and pointed at Monster. 'Out,' he said.

Monster opened both eyes, stretched, and wrapped his tail around his body. Terry groaned.

'Out,' Father repeated.

'It's beginning to snow,' said Tony.

'He'll freeze outside,' said Terry.

Before Father could say 'out' again, both boys stood up.

'We'll take him up to our room,' they said together. 'We promise he won't bother you tonight.'

Then, quickly, before Father could say anything, they scooped up the sleepy cat and ran upstairs.

'Good-night,' Mother called.

Father was still standing there with his mouth open, ready to repeat 'Out.'

Monster stretched out between Terry's and Tony's twin beds, purring loudly. He washed two grey paws and one ear, then gave up cleanliness for the evening. Terry looked at Tony. 'Do you really think he's worthless?' he asked.

'Kind of,' Tony answered. 'But I like him anyway.'

Tony checked to make sure the door was tightly shut. Then both boys went to sleep.

Tony heard the cat first, though Monster was on Terry's bed. As Tony sat up, he heard his brother mutter, 'Get off my head, you stupid cat.'

Monster jumped down and ran over to Tony, yowling as he streaked through the air.

Tony bent to pick him up, but Monster raced to the far corner of the room and began to scratch at the door.

'Get him quick, Terry,' Tony whispered. 'If he wakes Mum and Dad again, he'll be looking for a new home.'

Terry jumped out of bed and ran to the door. As he leaned over to pick up Monster, the cat slid from beneath him and ran to another corner.

Tony crawled out of bed and crept on hands and knees towards the runaway cat. Monster backed away and began to hiss and howl.

'Oh, no,' Terry groaned, and crawled over to help his twin.

'I bet he has to go outside,' Tony muttered.

Monster began to race around the room, jumping on the beds and chairs. Tony flicked on the light, and the boys began to back Monster under the desk. Tony reached him first.

Hissing, Monster arched his back. His eyes were wide open and glowing.

'What's wrong with him?' Tony asked.

'I don't know, but let's get him outside,' Terry replied.

As Tony opened their bedroom door, Monster under one arm, both boys suddenly stopped.

'Do you smell something?' asked Tony.

Terry sniffed. 'Is that smoke?'

Still grasping the yowling cat, Tony turned on the landing light. 'Go and get Mum and Dad. Quick!'

'What is that Monster up to now?' Father shouted.

'Fire!' yelled Tony, dialling the operator. Terry took Monster and headed for the stairway.

Father reached the telephone as Tony was giving their address. Then Mother came and all four raced outside with a strangely quiet Monster.

After the fire brigade had left, Mother set out hot chocolate and biscuits. Father sat at the kitchen table, stroking the purring cat.

'The firemen said there was very little damage,' Father told them. 'The wires were smouldering in the attic, but flames didn't have a chance to spread.'

Mother set a bowl of warm milk on the floor for Monster.

'What a cat!' she said. 'Do you think he really knew what he was doing?'

Monster opened his eyes, and slowly ambled over to the saucer of milk.

'I think so,' Tony said. 'He desperately wanted us to wake up.'

Monster began to eat biscuit crumbs.

'Monster still doesn't know he's a cat,' Father said.

'No,' Terry said. 'I think Monster believes he's a watchdog.'

'A watch*cat*,' Tony said, and they all laughed.

Wolf!

A True Story by Bev Ellen Clark

'THIS LOOKS LIKE a good place to camp,' Lyle Carter commented as he shrugged out of his rucksack.

'I guess it's as good as any,' his younger brother Raymond said. 'We can't go any farther tonight.'

'At least it's flat,' their cousin Tristan Belle commented as he kicked a large branch out of the way.

Tim Belle, ten, stood and watched his teenage brother and cousins with alarm. 'We're going to s-sleep here?' he stammered.

'Why not?' Lyle asked.

'I-I thought we were going to sleep in a cabin,' Tim quavered as he peered into the darkening woods around them.

'The cabin is still several miles from here,' Tristan, seventeen, explained. 'And it's already getting too dark to see the trail.'

'I guess we shouldn't have fooled around at that lake so long,' Raymond said, laughing.

'Oh, well. There's nothing like sleeping under the stars,' Lyle sighed contentedly as he flopped on top of his unrolled sleeping bag.

'But your dad said there were lots of wolves around this year,' Tim argued desperately.

'Oh, you know Dad,' Raymond said. 'He's always got some good wolf stories. What's wrong, Tim? Scared?'

'I'm not scared,' Tim declared, a little too quickly.

'I think your baby brother is afraid wolves will eat him out here,' Lyle said teasingly to Tristan.

'I am not!' Tim cried. 'It's just that there were two coyotes shot last week near here. Dad said they had rabies!'

Tristan stopped preparing his sleeping place and looked thoughtfully into the trees. Tim's cousins were silent. They all knew how dangerous a rabid animal could be. Most wild animals around there stayed away from people. But an animal with deadly rabies would attack fiercely, often for no apparent reason.

Tim blinked back tears. He had begged for weeks to be allowed to come with his big brother and cousins on this weekend backpacking trip. He was determined to show them he wasn't a 'baby'. He had done well, carrying his 35-pound pack all day and keeping up with the others' long-legged pace. But now he *was* scared.

Tim had always been more than a little afraid when his Uncle Ross told of the times he and other lumberjacks had met or had close calls with wolves and bears here in the wilds of Vancouver Island off the coast of British Columbia, Canada. Now his uncle's story of a rabid dog that had charged a man came back clearly.

Though neither Uncle Ross nor his two sons, Lyle and Raymond, believed in God or attended church as Tim and his family did, Tim knew his uncle was an honest man. The stories he told of his experiences in the woods were true.

Although it was a warm evening, Tim shivered as he unpacked his gear and unrolled his sleeping bag next to Tristan.

'Maybe we should build a lean-to or something,' he ventured hopefully.

'Why? It's not going to rain, and there's not a breath of wind,' Tristan said.

'Well then, can we at least have a campfire?' Tim pleaded.

'Ray, make a fire for this baby cousin of ours. I wouldn't mind some hot chocolate anyway,' Lyle said, still sprawled out lazily on his sleeping bag.

Soon a crackling fire threw out a bright, protective wall around the little circle. Tim actually felt quite safe and happy as he sipped hot cocoa with the others, and then snuggled down into his sleeping bag.

For a while he listened to the older boys talk about their summer jobs at the logging camp. But his shorter legs were tired and exhaustion soon claimed him.

It was cold and black when Tim woke up a few hours later. The fire was out and grey cottage-cheese clouds had smothered the stars. Tim raised himself up to search out the mounds of his sleeping companions but quickly dived back into his bag. He didn't like the looks of the giant trees reaching out for him with hairy arms.

Suddenly, an eerie howl froze Tim into a ball. He couldn't move a muscle as he listened to the howls and answering yaps coming from what seemed like several directions.

When his muffled moans brought no response from his brother, Tim burst out of his sleeping bag. 'Tristan! Tristan, listen!' he hissed.

'What?' Tristan asked sleepily.

'Listen—wolves!' Tim croaked.

Tristan lifted himself up a moment, then sank back into the warmth of his sleeping bag. 'They're miles from here, Timmy. Probably on the other side of the lake.'

'But, Tristan—'

'Go to sleep,' Tristan mumbled.

Go to sleep! How can I go to sleep? Tim wondered. *A pack of hungry wolves out there, maybe a rabid one, and us out in the open with nothing but sleeping bags for protection!*

Tim peered into the dark, looking for extra wood lying around the black circle where the fire had been. There wasn't any. And he certainly wouldn't go into the dark woods now by himself to get more.

'Tristan, shouldn't we build up the fire?' he asked. 'Tristan!'

It was no use. Tristan was either asleep or didn't want to be bothered again. If Tim forced his brother to wake up, he would just make him angry. Then there would be a scene with Tristan muttering about pesky baby brothers and how he should never have brought Tim along.

Tim tried to tell himself he was being silly. Why should he be afraid? Tristan didn't think there was anything to worry about. Those wolves could be miles away, and probably not rabid—but he couldn't stop shaking.

Remembering then that he hadn't prayed that night, Tim laid back and asked God to help him go back to sleep. 'And please, Lord, send some angels to protect us from the wolves,' he begged.

Thinking about angels reminded him of the Bible verse he had learned several weeks ago in Sunday school: 'The angel of the Lord encamps around those who fear him, and he delivers them' (Psalm 34:7).

Encamps around those who fear him, Tim thought, smiling. *It's just the right verse for tonight.*

Somehow, saying the verse over and over helped him feel better. As he pictured the angel of the Lord camping there beside them, he discovered he wasn't shaking any more.

The next thing Tim knew, the sun was shining in his eyes

and Raymond was noisily repacking his rucksack beside Tim. Propping himself up on his elbows and rubbing his eyes, Tim wiggled out of his sleeping bag as Lyle let out a whistle.

'Hey, guys, look at this!' he cried, dropping to his knees to study the dirt a short distance from where he had slept.

'Wow!' Tristan exclaimed.

'They're fresh tracks too,' Raymond said, looking down as he walked a slow circle around their camp. 'Looks like there was only one, but why would he come so close to us?'

'What?' Tim yelled, kicking free of his bag. 'What was it?'

'A wolf,' Lyle answered, standing up to stare around them into the woods. 'He came right into our camp last night. He must have been rabid to get this close to us.'

'What I'd like to know,' Raymond asked, 'is why he just walked in a circle around us.'

'The angel was here,' Tim said, looking down at the doglike tracks in the red, sandy soil.

'Angel? What are you talking about?' Lyle asked, looking from Tim to Tristan.

'The angel of the Lord encamps around those who fear him, and he delivers them,' Tim quoted. He didn't care if his cousins teased him this time. He smiled as he told them about his prayer.

The lighthearted joking of the previous day was missing now as the boys silently packed up and began the long trek homeward. When Timothy's cousins did finally start talking again, Tim noticed with a happy grin, they were asking Tristan about God and angels.

Names changed at the request of the author.

The Suitcase Bird

A Nature Story
by John Pedicord and Grace Anderson

IF YOU SEE A PELICAN in the zoo or on television, you may think, *How ugly! How clumsy!* The funny 'suitcase' under his bill makes him look double-chinned. And his short thick legs, big webbed feet, and pot-bellied body make him look awkward.

But if you first see him fly, first see his plummeting dive, first see him swim and fish, you won't think of him as ugly or awkward. Instead, you'll think power, speed, skill!

The brown pelican is the smallest pelican, weighing up to eight pounds with a wingspan of six and a half feet. But the white pelican may weigh up to twenty-four pounds with a wingspan up to ten feet. There are eight species in the world.

Pelicans live mainly in warm climates, though some breed in Canada. White pelicans breed inland. Brown pelicans are strictly seabirds, living on the coasts. Both breed in large groups, usually making nests on the ground though some nest in bushes and trees.

The mother pelican lays two to four chalky white eggs. Both parents sit on the eggs till the eggs hatch, about six weeks later. And both parents feed the young, bringing up partially digested food from their gullets into their pouches.

At first, they dribble this food into the chick's mouth. But when the chick is older, it sticks its head into a parent's pouch and feeds.

When the young are two weeks old, they leave their nests. They roam around in noisy bands, rushing at the adults when they come to feed them. But they are only fed by their own parents.

It is several weeks before the young birds have adult feathers and four years before they are ready to raise their own families. But then they may live as long as fifty-two years—or more!

God has given this interesting bird some unusual skills. White pelicans fish together in the water. Sometimes they form a line, beating the water with their wings and herding frightened fish into shallow water. Then they scoop up the fish with their pouches—and swallow it. (Their pouches are not for storage!)

The brown pelican dives from about twenty feet up, straight down into the water. His dive is so powerful that he can stun a fish six feet down and his dive may be heard half a mile away!

Pelicans have strong wings and great endurance. They can soar in the sky for hours without rest—as high as 8,000 feet! When flying in flocks, they form a V and beat their wings in unison. On record is a flight as fast as fifty-two miles per hour! Normally, however, they fly up to twenty-six miles per hour.

Around the turn of the century, the brown pelican's beautiful long feathers were in big demand for hats. So many were killed that the large brown bird was threatened with extinction.

In 1903 the American President, Teddy Roosevelt, set aside the first wildlife refuge in the United States. It is called Pelican Island and is off the coast of Florida.

Interestingly, the adult pelican is almost voiceless. But he makes his presence known by his unusual skills and strange appearance.

Yes, the pelican is one of God's more unusual creatures.

"AS SPOKESMAN FOR THE APARTMENT DWELLERS—"

A Horse Named 'Robert Raikes'

A True Story From the Nineteenth Century by Marie Manire Chapman

WHAT'S WRONG with this crazy horse? I didn't tell him to stop here!' The young man cracked his whip in the air to frighten the horse pulling his buggy. 'Giddap there, Raikes!' he cried.

But 'Robert Raikes', the horse, stood as calmly as if he were deaf to the sound of the whip. What he *did* hear were the voices of boys and girls shouting and laughing on their way home from school. When the first child had come into sight, the horse had stopped as quickly as though he'd heard, 'Whoa!'

'Giddap!' the red-faced driver shouted again. He glanced helplessly at the pretty girl seated beside him. 'It doesn't look as if we're going for much of a ride this afternoon. When I borrowed Raikes from Mr. Paxson, I thought he was a good horse. All his family think he's the best thing alive!'

Raikes tossed his mane and seemed to smile at the gathering children. The boys and girls noticed that the horse liked all the hugs and pats he was getting. And the children had no intention of leaving.

Suddenly the driver cleared his throat. 'Boys and girls, I

want to remind you to go to Sunday school when Sunday comes. I hope you're remembering to study your lessons faithfully. Now we must be on our way. Good day to you.'

He shook the reins and—sure enough—the little horse trotted happily down the road.

Stephen Paxson laughed when the young man returned the horse and told what had happened. Paxson explained, 'Robert Raikes is not just *any* horse; he's a missionary horse. Those boys and girls probably first heard about Sunday school from me while I was riding him! Even his name stands for Sunday school. He was named after Robert Raikes, the newspaper editor who started the first Sunday school in England.

Mr. Paxson himself learned to read and learned about the Lord Jesus in Sunday school. After he became a Christian, he rode horseback to other villages near his home in Winchester, Illinois, in the United States, and started more Sunday schools.

The American Sunday School Union (now called the American Missionary Fellowship) heard about his work. They needed a missionary in the Mississippi Valley. 'Will you be that missionary?' they asked. He accepted gladly.

The Paxson family moved from Winchester to Hickory Hills, Illinois, to be near the places that needed Sunday schools. They prayed for a stronger horse to carry Mr. Paxson—and God answered their prayers.

While away from home, Mr. Paxson found the horse. 'Look for a fourteen-stone man riding a sheep,' he wrote to his family. He came riding home on a small bay horse. It had a long neck and body and a blaze (white mark) on its face. Mr. Paxson was so tall that his feet almost touched the ground on each side.

For twenty-five years, the funny-looking little animal carried or pulled Mr. Paxson on his travels. Raikes also carried Mr. Paxson's supplies and books for the new Sunday schools.

On one trip, the horse needed new shoes. The blacksmith heard the words *Sunday school* and told Mr. Paxson, 'I was an orphan. When I was young I had to help a blacksmith and never had a chance to go to school.

'Then when I was nineteen, a man came to our town and started a Sunday school. I went to the Sunday school and learned to read, and I heard about Jesus for the first time. Now I'm a Christian, and I owe everything to that man.'

'I am that man,' Mr. Paxson said, smiling, 'and the horse you are shoeing is the very horse that brought me to your town.'

'I won't take any money for shoeing him!' cried the blacksmith. 'Any time he needs shoes and you're near here, bring him to me. I will shoe him all his life for nothing.'

Missionary and horse went through many hardships and all kinds of weather. Once they came to the edge of a big mudhole. The horse stopped. Paxson got out of the buggy and told the horse to go ahead.

All went well till they came upon a dead ox in the middle of the hole. The horse got scared and tried to run. When Paxson tried to catch the horse, his boots got stuck in the mud. He had to reach down and pull them out.

When he looked around for Raikes, the little horse was standing on firm ground looking at him and making a noise as if to say, 'Come on, Friend. I made it. Surely you can too!'

Robert Raikes carried his master over 100,000 miles and became famous. A picture of him was a favourite prize for Sunday school pupils. When he could no longer carry his master, he was lovingly cared for by the family while Mr. Paxson continued his travels on another horse.

When Raikes died, many newspapers printed a story about the horse that helped start 700 Sunday schools. Mr. Paxson cried that day in October, 1868, when he read the letter from his daughter Mary telling about Raikes' death. She said, 'Dear Father, I sat down to tell you of the death of your old servant, Robert Raikes. While looking at the remains of this faithful creature, I could not but ask myself, *Am I as faithful to my heavenly Master as he has been to his earthly one?*'

Robert Raikes was more than a horse ridden by a missionary; he was really a missionary horse.

Deadly Eddie

A True Story from America
by Irene Aiken

I HAD JUST COME HOME from school. As I stepped into my room, a reddish brown, three-foot snake slithered out from under my chest of drawers. He stopped and stared unblinking at me, and I stood frozen to the spot.

'Motherrrrr!' I screamed.

'It's only Eddie,' came Mother's calm voice. 'Marie is here. She brought along her pet snake for Lloyd's birthday.'

Marie, my country cousin, had no fear of snakes, toads, snails, or worms. At eleven, I hated them all.

Just then my brother, who was seven that day, came running into my room. 'You'll scare the life out of him with that screaming,' he said, giving me a withering look. 'C'mon, Eddie, I'll put you back in your aquarium.'

Just then Marie poked her head in the room. 'Oh, this is where he got to,' she said, laughing.

Eddie went into a 'cute' act then, drawing himself into a coil and blowing himself up like a balloon. His head flattened too, making him look like a cobra.

'He's a hognose snake, perfectly harmless,' Marie said as Lloyd tried to grab him.

'He looks deadly,' I said, keeping my distance.

'He likes to play dead too,' she said and poked at the snake. Eddie immediately rolled over and lay all stiffened out.

'Wait till you see him change his skin,' Marie added. 'That's a real show.'

I shook my head at her. 'You brought my brother a snake for his birthday? Couldn't you have found a baseball or a toy truck or something?'

'But Eddie is completely harmless!' she cried. 'I wanted to show you all what happens when he changes his skin. It's so much like what happened to me last week. I went to special services at church and received Jesus as my Saviour. I'm not the same Marie you knew before.'

I didn't see how receiving Jesus could have anything to do with Eddie changing his skin, so I changed the subject. 'Don't you have to feed snakes live food—like mice? Or toads? Where will we find them?'

'Oh, I brought along a boxful of toads. Five, in fact.'

Marie was laughing. 'Lloyd has already given one to Eddie.'

I made a face and shuddered, but in the next few days, I grew used to Eddie being in the aquarium—with his mesh cover fastened down tight.

A couple of weeks later, Eddie began to look sick and we all worried about him—even me. Eddie was lying in the corner of his baking pan swimming pool, looking dull and greyish. His eyes clouded over and it was easy to see that he was dying.

My two brothers and I, even our parents, stood around a lot, gazing at his still form.

'Best birthday present I ever had, but I guess I'll have to set him free,' Lloyd said sadly. 'In the park, maybe.'

'Here I trapped a field mouse for him,' I said. 'Maybe that will perk him up.' I opened the little trap door carefully and, with a shudder, dropped the live grey mouse into the aquarium. I didn't like mice any better than snakes, but I hated to see a mouse swallowed whole.

I needn't have worried. Eddie ignored the mouse, and we had to fish it out.

Three days passed, with Eddie looking deader every day. (Lloyd hadn't let him go.) Then I recalled Marie's words: 'Wait till you see him change his skin.'

'Maybe this is all the way it's supposed to be,' I told my brother. 'Maybe he's changing his skin.'

The next day I had barely come into the house when Lloyd was dragging me by the hand to his room. 'Renie, you were right. You've got to see what Eddie is doing! His face is peeling off!'

Eddie was swaying back and forth like snakes you see being hypnotized. As he swayed, his old skin pulled back and he emerged, looking at us through sparkling black-bead eyes.

All sleek and pretty—in brushed-red and orange and amber—he moved away from the old skin without looking back. Now he was ready for that mouse. Lucky mouse—set free some time before!

I stood there looking at Eddie and thinking about what Marie had said—how Eddie's losing his old skin was like her getting saved and getting rid of her sins. Now I understood what she meant. A Bible verse I had memorized described it perfectly: 'If anyone is in Christ, he is a new creation; the old has gone, the new has come!' (2 Corinthians 5:17).

Yes, Eddie was a pretty good example. I had received Jesus myself. In a sense *my* 'old skin' had fallen away too, and I had come out brand new.

I could hardly wait to tell a friend of mine at school who needed to 'change her skin'. In fact, I asked Lloyd if I could have Eddie's old skin to show her.

Of course, I'd have to tell her that receiving Jesus would not mean she'd be perfect. Even with a new skin, Eddie was hard on mice and toads.

It was kind of hard to explain how a person could be all brand new, yet need to go to Jesus for forgiveness each day. But thanks to Marie and her 'weird' birthday gift, our entire family now had a living picture of Marie's new life in Jesus— a picture we could share in turn with friends.

Sly Thief

by Gloria A. Truitt

I'm quite a clever animal
   That's known for sly escapes.
Into the vineyards I would sneak
   To steal the juicy grapes.
Within the Book of Luke it tells
   How Christ compared me to
An evil king called Herod who
   Was wicked through and through.
I make my home in burrows or
   In holes among the rocks,
And scavenge for my food at night
   For I'm that cunning fox!

(Luke 13:32)

Largest
of the Apes

by Gloria A. Truitt

Unlike my monkey relatives,
  A treetop's not my home.
Instead, the Congo forest land
  Is where I like to roam.

I make a nest of twigs and leaves
  And sleep upon the ground,
Eating ferns, bananas, and
  What berries can be found.

Like you, I have a family.
  We never live apart.
I'm peaceful and good-natured, and
  I'm known to be quite smart.

I can weigh 600 pounds,
  My height can reach six feet,
So if you saw me in a zoo
  You'd not say I'm petite!

Folks call me Big Gorilla, and
  I'm sure you will agree
That in the *great ape* family
  There are none compared to me!

The Fox Watch

A True Story by Margaret Lacey

IN IOWA IN THE USA there are no mountains, but there are large piles of pink shale left by coal miners who finished their job and went away. One of those piles of shale was my own special pink mountain. It was about 150 feet high and stood in the middle of the large field our neighbour's used for cows. He let me visit the mountain whenever I wanted to.

The nicest thing about 'my mountain' was that it was a home for foxes. But though I always visited their holes when I climbed the shale pile, I had never seen a fox.

One summer evening when I was ten, I asked my mother, 'May I sleep on top of the shale pile tonight? Uncle Russell says that just before the sun comes up is the best time to see a fox.'

Mum looked a bit scared. But since she was very understanding, she said, 'All right, but be sure to get there before dark. And if the bull is with the cows, you know you have to be careful.'

'Yippee!' I shouted. 'Thanks, Mum!' And I ran upstairs to find the old blankets we used when we slept outside. I decided not to take my pyjamas, but I did think I might need my clock.

'What time does the sun come up, Mum?' I yelled. 'I want to set my alarm clock.'

She laughed, and said, 'The alarm will scare away the foxes.'

'But what if I oversleep?' I asked.

'OK,' Mum said. 'Set it for about five o'clock. Then you should be ready for the foxes.'

I rolled the alarm clock, my torch, and a bag of biscuits inside my blankets, tied the roll with clothesline, and hung it over one shoulder. 'Good-bye, Mum; good-bye, Dad,' I said. 'I'll be back in the morning.'

It was still broad daylight when I started on my walk. I climbed the fence from our lane into our neighbour's field.

I didn't have any shoes on, but the soles of my feet were so tough in the summer that I hardly ever got cut. When I stopped for a minute, something tickled my toes, and I was surprised to find I was standing on a little garter snake. Carefully, I picked him up right behind his head and watched his forked tongue go in and out of his mouth. How beautiful his back was!

I carried the little snake as I walked on. When I came to the stream which wandered around until it finally led to the foot of my mountain, I let him go beside the water. In a moment he had disappeared.

I sat beside the stream for a while. When the water got quiet I could see striped minnows about half an inch long swimming around. I even saw some crayfish that looked like tiny brown lobsters. When they got scared, they moved into their holes so fast, my eyes could hardly follow them.

As I walked along, redwing blackbirds scolded me. I knew their nests were nearby, and they were trying to keep their eggs or babies safe from me, so I decided not to stop and make them worry more.

The field had many special places in it. One was the little hill, just ahead, where moss with red flowers grew. The moss made a lovely pillow because it was so soft.

I climbed the hill and from the top I could finally see the shale pile. In the setting sun, it looked beautiful—as red as fire. I had never seen it so late in the evening.

When I started out again, I had to make a detour around some reeds with sharp edges. If I walked through them, I would get cuts all over my arms and legs like the paper cuts I sometimes got at school.

But finally I reached the base of my pink mountain. I decided to go up the steepest side as usual because I felt like a mountain climber. I dug my bare feet into the soft shale and didn't slip once as I climbed. When I finally stood up on the flat top, I could see a long way.

Back to the west were our barn and silo. I couldn't see the house because it was hidden by the barn. Below me, the redwing blackbirds still scolded. A hawk circled high overhead. Each time she came around, she was lower. I think she hoped to have blackbird for dinner.

Far to the southeast I could see something blue. It was a patch of flowers called blue flag. I remembered that Mum always liked me to bring some home, so I decided to do that in the morning.

In the east, the field was filled with little trees with long sharp thorns. They were locust trees and were a favourite home for birds called shrikes. The shrikes hung dead songbirds and mice on the thorns until they were ready to eat them.

Along the fence to the north stood the only tall trees in the field. In one of them the hawk had her big messy nest. I wondered if she had any babies to feed. Under the trees I could see our neighbour's cows, but the bull wasn't with them. He must have been in his pen at home.

Since it was starting to get dark, I knew I had to find a flat place to put my blankets. First, I visited the fox holes. There were lots of them, but some were empty. The chicken bones and feathers in front of them told me which were being used.

I found traps in two of the holes and put sticks in them to make them snap shut. Our neighbour hated the foxes because they sometimes ate his chickens, but I always set off the traps anyway.

Were the foxes at home or had they gone hunting, I wondered. If they heard me, they were probably frightened. I got down and whispered into the holes, 'Don't be afraid; I won't hurt you. I'm just going to sleep here.'

While smoothing out a place for my bed, I found a lot of flat stones to skim on the water below. I decided to wait till morning for that too. One piece of pink shale had a fossil leaf in it. I put that in my pocket to show my parents.

After getting under my blanket, I felt a bit lonely and remembered that Mother had looked scared when I asked if I could sleep out. It didn't help when something said, 'Oooooo,' just then. I decided it was a big owl.

Then I remembered seeing cattle tracks up there and hoped that if any cows came up during the night, they wouldn't step on me. It helped to have the alarm clock ticking beside me. As I listened to it, I fell asleep.

Something woke me up just before the alarm went off. I lay looking up at the sky. Some stars were still out, but it was getting light. What had awakened me? As I lay there wondering, I heard a funny noise down the hill from me. It sounded like a sharp bark.

Suddenly, I was wide awake. The foxes were coming

home! I started to jump up but remembered that I would scare them. So I turned over very carefully and crawled on my stomach to the edge of the hill, just above the holes.

There they were—a father, mother, and three pups! I couldn't be sure, but I thought it must be the father who came first. His ears stood up straight and he sniffed the air. He had a chicken feather hanging from his ruff.

The mother fox watched the babies to make sure they didn't stray as they made side trips and detours. She said, 'Yip!' whenever one of them went off too far.

I thought they would go into their holes right away. Instead, they came straight up to the top of the shale pile. The wind must have been blowing from behind them so they hadn't caught my scent.

I was so excited I was shaking, but I tried to make myself look like a rock. They were close enough now for me to see the markings on their fur. It gave me a shivery feeling to look at their eyes. They weren't like my dog's eyes—but more like the eyes of *wolves*.

Suddenly the father fox saw me. He looked so surprised I almost giggled. I could tell he was more scared than I was. He gave a special bark and in an instant the whole family disappeared into a hole.

I stayed still for several minutes, but I knew I wouldn't see them again.

I didn't stop to think about how early it was. Quickly, I rolled the torch and clock into my bedroll, leaving the biscuits for the foxes. I ran down the side of my pink mountain in big, happy leaps.

It was only when I got halfway home that I remembered my plans to skim stones and pick blue flags for Mum. But I didn't go back. I was in too big a hurry to get home and tell my parents about the foxes.

Look, Mum— No Hands!

A Nature Story
by Grace Fox Anderson

IF YOU'VE WATCHED trained seals perform, you know what clever, lovable creatures they are. It's amazing what the trained seal (usually a sea lion cow) can do without hands—only flippers.

It can balance a ball or other item on its nose as it waddles up and down steps. It can toss a ball to its trainer and catch it again on its nose. It can even play a simple tune on a series of horns.

God has made the seal a natural clown. Fun-loving and curious, wild seals will follow a boat just to listen to the odd sounds it makes. Wild sea lion cows have been seen playing with seaweed or driftwood. They will toss it in the air, dive under it—even toss it back and forth to each other.

Their strong flippers and streamlined bodies make them graceful swimmers and excellent divers. They can dive as deep as 200 feet, stay under water as long as 30 minutes, and swim on their backs or stomachs.

The seal's normally friendly nature makes it easy to train. However, the seal is also easy for hunters to kill. Eskimos out hunting seals simply walk among them and club the young males on the head. Seals are killed for meat, blubber, and fur. Other seal-enemies are sharks, killer whales, and polar bears.

Altogether there are thirty kinds of seals. They are divided into two groups—those with visible ears and those with invisible ears.

Sea lions and fur seals have visible ears. True seals such as leopard and elephant seals have invisible ears. Also, the sea lion's back flippers are more like legs than the flippers of the true seal.

Though they are warm-blooded *mammals*, most seals are found in cool water. God has given the seal a layer of fat or blubber under the skin to keep him warm. And his entire body is covered with hair.

Seals come in different sizes. The Siberian freshwater seal is only three feet long. An elephant seal can be eighteen feet long!

Seal sounds are varied too. They may growl and bark or roar or cry or 'sing'.

Some seals, like the sea lion, live in big groups. Others, like the harbour seal, live in small family groups of one male and two or three females and their pups.

They are all meat-eaters, eating fish, squid, lobster, or shrimp. Some eat other warm-blooded animals such as penguins.

The female is able to bear young when she is three years old. She has one pup a year. The newborn seal looks much like a furry young dog. It is often white, grows fast, and cries like a human baby.

Sea lion pups are poorly cared for. The mother may leave her youngster all day while she goes off to feed. Other females will cuff it away and fighting bulls may crush it. The pup is quite helpless and must be taught to swim by the mother.

I hope you have a chance to see God's flippered sea clown perform. If you do, I'm sure you'll agree she's a natural, lovable show-off.

" YOU'VE BEEN AWFULLY QUIET, JOHN, EVER SINCE WE RAN INTO THAT BIG LOG "

The Secret
of Tawachi
Mountain

A Fiction Story by Corrine Bergstrom

BILLY STRAIGHT ARROW and Joe Moreno fell to their knees beside the spring gushing into the mountain stream. They each took a long drink of clear water, then Joe straightened up.

'Well, are you coming with me or not?' Joe asked impatiently.

Billy sat up and stared at the top of Tawachi Mountain. His parents said that the fire god lived there. At the mission school, he had learned that there was only one God, a God of love. But a shiver ran through him anyway.

He realized he would have to climb the mountain. He didn't want Joe to think him a coward. Joe, who was part Indian, came from a Christian family. They didn't fear the mountain as Billy's family did.

'Wait for me,' he called to Joe who had already started to climb.

Perhaps, if Billy could tell his parents he had been on top of Tawachi, they wouldn't fear the fire god. Maybe then they'd listen to the pastor from the mission church when he told of the one and only God and His Son Jesus.

The boys climbed quickly, rocks tumbling beneath their feet. At the top they stopped, breathless. Billy scanned the horizon. He could see mile after mile of valleys and ridges. It made him feel strangely powerful. 'Look, Joe!' he shouted, pointing to the south. 'An eagle.'

Joe turned. 'Yeah,' he murmured, awe in his voice. 'A bald eagle. See his white head?'

They watched the bird glide gracefully around the mountaintop. It turned suddenly and swooped down, not far from the boys.

'Let's find its nest,' Billy whispered. Joe grinned in agreement.

Quickly and quietly they made their way through the tall vegetation.

Suddenly, Billy motioned for Joe to stop. 'Listen,' he mouthed. Joe paused and cocked his ear; then he nodded. They could hear a shrill chirping.

They moved slowly forward. Finally they spotted the eagle's huge nest, perched high between two rocks. The chirping noise was made by three fuzzy eaglets.

'Babies,' Joe whispered excitedly.

Billy watched, fascinated. The young birds looked much like baby chicks, covered with soft white down. It did not seem possible that they would grow as large and beautiful as their parents.

'Let's go,' he motioned. They moved away as quietly as they had come.

It was late when the boys reached the foot of the mountain. They made plans to see each other at a Scout meeting the next day, then separated.

Billy's parents were angry at his late arrival. When he told them where he had been, fear filled their eyes. 'The fire god, he did not bother you?' his father asked.

Billy shook his head. 'There is no fire god, Father. It is as the pastor at the mission has tried to tell our people.'

'This I do not believe,' his father replied. 'Over the years many of our people have been lost to the fire god on Tawachi. When he breathes his flames, they never return. You must not climb Tawachi again!' his father insisted.

Billy felt sad. Even after he had shown his parents that nothing had happened, they still believed that there was a fire god. He had tried many times to explain that the true God was a living Person—not a spirit god to scare you like the Indian gods.

The next day, Billy listened excitedly as Mr. Jackson, the Boy Scout leader, told about their annual Scout festival. He said that an eagle's feather was needed for their display.

'A feather from the bald eagle would be most valuable, but this species of eagle is almost extinct,' Mr. Jackson continued. 'A few of the birds have been sighted in nearby mountains. None have been seen recently, however.'

Billy was bursting to tell about the nest he and Joe had discovered, but he knew they must keep it a secret to protect the birds.

He glanced at Joe who was trying to attract Mr. Jackson's attention. 'No, Joe, we cannot tell the secret of Tawachi Mountain,' he whispered to his friend.

Joe looked puzzled, but nodded agreement. When they were alone, he asked, 'Why couldn't I tell Mr. Jackson where to find an eagle's feather?'

'Because we don't want anyone to harm the birds or their nest,' Billy explained.

Joe's eyes brightened. 'OK, I see now. Mr. Jackson said there weren't many eagles any more. But that doesn't mean we can't get the feather ourselves, does it?'

'No. But—' Billy faltered. 'I can't go. My father has forbidden me to climb Tawachi again.'

Joe understood. 'I'll go alone,' he said.

'OK,' Billy agreed. 'I'll wait for you at the stream.'

The sun was high and hot when the boys reached the rippling stream the next day.

It was not long before Joe disappeared from sight. Billy looked up, shading his eyes with his hand. He couldn't see his friend on the mountain or the eagle in the sky.

A jeep full of noisy teenagers passed him. Billy noted with disgust that two of them were smoking. 'Hey, Andy, can this heap climb that mountain?' one of the teens called to the driver.

In answer, the driver revved the motor. The jeep spurted to the right where a jeep trail, almost hidden, wound between the scrub pine. Billy hoped they'd return on the other side of the mountain. Soon everything was quiet again.

Billy drank from the spring, then tried to catch a lizard that slithered between the rocks. He even took a nap.

When he woke up, he gazed upwards, frowning. The sun was far to the west. Joe should have returned by now.

Billy wrinkled his nose. What was that smell? His heart beat wildly. It was the unmistakable smell of fire!

The fire god! Billy shook his head at his first wild thought. No, there was no fire god! Maybe the boys in the jeep had built a campfire. Yes, that must be it.

But the pungent odour grew stronger, and Billy heard the fierce roar of a forest fire. He remembered the boys' cigarettes. They could have accidentally started the fire.

And Joe. Joe was on top of Tawachi! Was he trapped by the fire?

Without a second thought, Billy began to climb. The air grew hotter and hotter. Deer ran from between the trees. Birds flew overhead, scolding loudly. Was the proud eagle one of them?

Billy pushed on. Smoke filled his lungs. He could hardly breathe. He stopped and tied his handkerchief around his nose and mouth.

Soon small flames danced before him, then larger ones. Billy wormed his way between them. Higher and higher he climbed.

He called, 'Joe! Joe!' But there was no answer. Finally he

reached the top of Tawachi. He located the eagles' nest without much trouble, but found no sign of his friend.

The baby birds were crying weakly. Their beaks opened and shut slowly, as they gasped for air. Billy broke away the piece of nest where the eaglets lay and hugged it to him. He couldn't leave the birds to die.

But when he turned around and saw that the blaze had closed in from behind, he panicked. Would he die here with the birds?

Then his thoughts turned to his strong Saviour, Jesus. At the mission school, Billy had learned that Jesus would also be his Helper and Guide. He prayed as he had never prayed before, and his pounding heart calmed.

The jeep trail! The one he had hoped the boys in the jeep would take down the other side of the mountain. Maybe he could escape that way. It would be to the right of him now.

He stumbled in that direction, almost losing the nest. He stopped and got a better grip on his precious load, then plodded on. Suddenly a new sensation filled his lungs. Fresh air! The young birds felt it too. One even let out a feeble chirp.

The fire was behind Billy now. He had followed the ruts of the jeep trail without any trouble.

Finally, he sat down at the foot of the mountain, exhausted. He grinned at the birds as he placed them beside him. 'With God's help, we made it,' he told them.

But what had become of Joe?

A whirring noise overhead caught Billy's attention. A helicopter headed straight into the heart of the flames. Another followed. 'That must be the rescue service,' Billy decided. 'They'll find Joe if anyone can.'

He picked up the nest and got to his feet. Already the eaglets missed their mother. They cheeped and chirped, working their mouths open and closed. They must be hungry. But what did baby eagles eat?

By now his parents would know he had disobeyed them. He'd hurry home and explain. He could leave the birds with them while he found out about Joe.

'Billy! Billy!' a voice called in the distance. 'Billy!' He heard other voices, but that first one brought joy to his heart. It was Joe's. His friend was alive!

'I'm here,' Billy shouted. Then he saw them. Joe, slightly dishevelled, but safe; Joe's father; and his own father too.

'The baby eagles! You have them!' Joe shouted happily. 'When I saw the smoke from the fire, I forgot about them and ran. I knew I couldn't return the way I came. I prayed for God to help me. Then I heard the jeep going down the mountainside, and I went that way.'

Billy's father moved to his side. 'My son, you disobeyed me,' he said sternly. But Billy recognized something else in his voice. His father was thankful that he was safe.

'Yes, Father.' Billy hung his head. 'But I only did it to save my friend.'

'From the fire god,' his father added.

'No, Father,' Billy began, wanting so hard for his father to understand. 'The boys in the jeep had cigarettes and must have started the fire. The one and only God helped me find the jeep trail. Without Him, I would have been lost in the fire.'

Billy's father stared up at Tawachi, now shrouded in smoke. 'This God must be strong, more powerful than the fire god.'

'Yes, Father,' Billy spoke softly. It was a beginning. Later he would explain more.

'The birds,' Joe interrupted. 'What will we do with them?'

'I'll take them home with me for now,' Billy said. 'When

the fire dies, we must return them to Tawachi to their mother.' He looked straight into his father's eyes. 'May I go back with Joe?'

His father nodded. 'You may go.'

Joe, grinning widely, held up a long feather. Billy said, 'We must still keep the secret of Tawachi Mountain to protect the birds. They may be the last of their kind.'

Joe and the two fathers nodded solemnly.

My Friends, the Wrens

A Nature Story by L. M. Smith

DID YOU KNOW that birds behave very much like people? Well, I didn't until I moved to the country. A friend gave me a gourd and told me how to turn it into a wren house.

I made it according to his directions and hung it on the porch. In a few days, two wrens began to build a nest in it. First they carried in small twigs and grass. Then they lined it with feathers and fuzz.

In a couple of weeks, baby wrens hatched. I could tell because I saw Mother Wren drop the broken egg shells out of the nest. They were a dull white with brown freckles.

All day long Father and Mother Wren flew back and forth, taking food to their babies. About two weeks later, the parents coaxed one young bird out of their house. Scolding and coaxing, they got it to follow them and taught it to fly short distances.

The baby bird left in the gourdhouse was impatient. He put his head out the door and cried, 'Yeep-yeep-yeep!'

Mother bird came and scolded him back into the house. Then she flew back to the other baby.

'Yeep-yeep-yeep,' came again from the house, and the baby stuck his head out.

This time Mother Wren gave him a peck on the head and went inside the house with him. (Just think, God gave mother wrens the wisdom to take care of their young just as He gives human mothers wisdom.)

Mother Wren stayed inside a long time while the father gave the other baby its flying lesson. I wondered if Mother Wren was telling her baby about cats that hide in the grass, just waiting to catch a baby bird.

Wouldn't you know it, as soon as Mother Wren left, that disobedient baby bird came out of the house and tumbled right to the ground. And sure enough a cat darted from behind some bushes and grabbed it.

Poor baby bird! He spread his little wings as far as he could and yeeped for his parents.

I rushed out of the house, picked up a stick, and gave the cat a good whack. It let go of the baby bird and ran off down the garden. Then the bird hopped into some nearby bushes.

Afterwards, I couldn't help but remember the Bible verse, 'Children, obey your parents in the Lord, for this is right' (Ephesians 6:1).

The Runaway Cow

A True Story by Pat Wayne

DAD STOOD in our living room doorway and repeated his question: 'What happened to Number Thirteen? I can't find her anywhere.'

'What?' I asked. 'After school I fed all the cows that came for hay. *Thirteen* didn't come. I just thought maybe she liked grass better than hay.'

We call our cows by the numbers on their ear tags. They are not milk cows, but are brown-and-white Herefords.

Mum came from the kitchen. She had on an apron over her dress and flour on her nose. Tonight, one of Mum's nights to cook, was chicken pie night. 'Can't you find Thirteen?' she asked, worried.

'Is Thirteen missing?' asked Timmy, my seven-year-old brother. 'She was here yesterday. I remember.'

'I know,' I said. It sounds stupid to get upset over a cow—but to know Thirteen is to love her. She is different in that she loves not only her calves; she helps protect *all* the calves!

Mother looked at Dad and Dad looked at me and I looked at Timmy. We all knew what was wrong with Thirteen.

'You took her calf,' Timmy said to Dad. 'You took *all* the calves.'

'We had to sell them,' Dad said. 'That's the way we make money, Timmy. But you're probably right. The truck picked up the calves this morning. Thirteen is probably out somewhere hunting for them.'

'I don't think I want to live in the country any more,' Timmy said.

'I do!' I said quickly. I remembered the city where we used to live—the rushing crowds and the sound of police cars. 'I plan to study agriculture some day, and I hope to be a vet.'

I thought about our rolling green acres—200 of them— and the streams and huge, spring-fed pond where we could fish or swim. I thought of the tall, whispering pines, lined up in rows as if protecting our white house and red barn.

'I like it here too,' Mum said.

Timmy sniffed. 'I want Thirteen back. She is my favourite. She lets me make a fuss of her and she knows I won't hurt her calves because I told her.'

'How far can a cow go without someone noticing her?' Mum asked.

'We'll check our farm tonight,' Dad said. 'Tomorrow evening after work—if we haven't found her—we'll take both cars and look.'

The next evening Dad drove the truck and I jumped out and asked at each farm. We called home twice to see if Mum and Timmy had found Thirteen, but there was no answer. No one we talked to had seen our cow.

It was almost dark when Dad turned down the lane where a new couple lived. 'I heard that Mr. and Mrs. Johnson have retired here,' he told me.

As we bumped down the lane, we caught a glimpse of one

little light. Dad stopped the truck and we both got out. He reached for his torch.

A porch light went on and a lady came to the door. 'Hello,' she called.

'We live four miles back up the main road,' Daddy said.

'I'm so glad to see someone,' the lady said as we walked up the porch steps. 'My husband was taken ill and had to go to the hospital. My car has broken down and is in the garage. I walked home tonight from the bus on the main road. I don't know anyone yet.'

'You have some help now,' Daddy told her gently. 'If you'll get me a new bulb, I'll climb up and see if that will fix your yard light. Tomorrow morning my wife can take you to the garage to see if your car is ready. If not, I'll come to the garage and drive you to the hospital.'

'Oh, my,' the lady said. 'My name is Minnie Johnson, and I really do thank you.'

'I'm Dan Peterson. This is my daughter Becky,' Daddy said. 'We are only being neighbourly. You have good neighbours. How is your husband doing?'

'My Henry is doing really well. The doctor said he'd be able to come home this weekend.' We followed her into the house as she talked. She went to the kitchen and got a light bulb.

'We're looking for a missing cow,' I told her as Dad took the bulb and went out in the yard.

'We only have little calves,' Mrs. Johnson said. 'I haven't fed them yet tonight. That's always Henry's job. The yard light will be a big help.'

'I'll help you feed them,' I offered.

'My, that will be nice,' she said. 'I've been keeping them in the barn and farmyard since Henry's been ill. Our fence needs repairing, so I was afraid they'd wander off.'

'Fences always need work done on them,' I said. 'There goes the light. Wow, that really lights up the yard.'

Dad came pounding up the front steps. 'Becky,' he called, 'guess who is in the barn with Mrs. Johnson's calves?'

'Thirteen!' I yelled, and dashed out the door.

Mrs. Johnson followed me, exclaiming, 'Well, I never! You found thirteen cows?'

Dad explained it all to Mrs. Johnson as I ran to the barn, blinking back tears. 'Number Thirteen!' I shouted at her. She was sitting calmly among the calves. She stood and bellowed, 'Moo' at me.

I rubbed her funny, furry face. 'You found some new calves to adopt, huh?' I said. I looked at the three calves in the hay. We always talk to our cows, and they always answer in their way.

Thirteen said, 'Moo,' and snorted a little.

'I'm sorry about selling your calf,' I said. 'That's a part of life you have to accept.'

Mrs. Johnson sighed as she and Dad came into the barn. 'My, I didn't realize how much work there would be on a farm. Henry always wanted to retire with a piece of ground.'

'Do you like it here?' I asked her. 'You have the best cherry trees in the valley. People come from miles around and pay to pick your cherries. That will be an extra income for you. You have a really pretty view of the hills too.'

'I know,' she said. 'I guess I'm just upset because Henry's not here and everything is so new.'

'Daddy, maybe Thirteen could stay with Mrs. Johnson's calves until the weekend,' I suggested.

Dad nodded. 'I'll come this weekend and help mend your fence. My wife bakes good pies, and we'll bring some food over for your husband's homecoming.'

Mrs. Johnson had tears in her eyes. 'I don't know how to thank you.'

'Mum always says to pass on the kindness,' I said. 'There will be someone who needs your help sometime.'

I turned to Thirteen. 'You can stay here until the weekend. Then you'd better come home.' I rubbed her face and gave her a hug. 'We want you home,' I said. 'Number One will be having a calf this week, and Number Four is due soon. And it won't be too long before you'll have another calf of your own.'

Number Thirteen answered with a loud 'Moo'.

Farmyard Fatty

by Gloria A. Truitt

Farmers feed me lots of corn
   So I'll grow fat and chubby.
And though I like to roll in mud,
   You wouldn't say I'm grubby.
This mud keeps insects off my skin,
   And cools me when it's hot.
But still my bed of straw will be
   The farmyard's cleanest spot.
Food for your table I provide,
   Like bacon, pork, and ham,
For I'm a farmyard *fatty*—
   A pig! That's what I am!

The Christmas Trap

A Fiction Story by Carole DeSoto

CONNIE WALKER HURRIED past the Christmas tree in the living room and opened the door. Still no Reggie waiting to leap at her off the picnic table. 'Here, Reggie! Here, Reg!' she called. But there was no sign of her striped tiger cat.

Connie shivered as she watched the large snowflakes float down. The garden was covered with snow already. At least it would be a white Christmas!

She slowly closed the door and looked up to see her mother standing beside her. 'He'll come back, Dear,' her mother said. 'Tomcats like to wander.'

'But, Mum, he's been gone for two days. Reggie has never done that before.'

'Did you check next door with Mr. Aucker to see if Reggie had come to the kennel?'

Connie shook her head.

'Well, after breakfast why don't you run over and ask? Anyway, Mr. Aucker will be glad of your help. I'm sure he'll have a lot of animal boarders on Christmas Eve,' Mother said.

Connie looked at her bacon and eggs with little appetite. She couldn't help but see the stocking she'd hung by the fireplace for Reggie. Last year he himself had been a squirming ball of fur in her stocking—with just his head sticking out. Tears rolled down her cheeks.

'Have you talked to God about Reggie?' her mother asked across the table. 'Why don't you ask the blessing for the food and pray for Reggie too?'

'Do you think God would care—about a cat, I mean?' Connie asked.

'He cares about everything that concerns us—and of course He cares about His creatures,' her mother answered. 'Remember what Jesus said about sparrows? He knows if just one falls' (Matthew 10:29).

Connie bowed her head and asked the blessing. Then she added, 'Please watch over Reggie, Lord. He's not used to being out in cold weather like this. And may he come home for Christmas. He's the only present I want.'

When she looked up, she asked, 'Do you really think God will send him back, Mum?'

'Well, God doesn't always answer our prayers the way we'd like or when we'd like Him to. But I'm sure He's watching over Reggie.'

Connie smiled for the first time that day.

'I have to go to the office for a few hours to finish one more project, Connie. Will you be all right?'

'Sure,' Connie said. 'I'll go over to Mr. Aucker's and see if Reggie has been there.'

'And if you'll set the table and prepare the potatoes for tonight, that will be a big help,' Mrs. Walker said.

Connie pulled her coat tight as she hurried over to Aucker's Animal Hospital. She was glad the Auckers would be coming to dinner tonight. She missed her father, who had died two years before. Mr. Aucker was older, but he was kind and loved to play with Reggie.

'Hi, Mr. Aucker,' Connie greeted the veterinarian as she walked into his examination room.

'Hello there, Connie. You're just in time to give me a hand. Try to calm this puppy while I put ice on his swollen paw,' he said.

'What happened to him?' Connie asked.

'The little fellow got caught in a trap. Jim Back is setting his fur traps too close to the homes around here,' he said.

'Why does he do that?' Connie asked.

'He's just an old man who's got lazy. He puts the traps closer to his house so he won't have to walk so far to check them.'

'But he's trapping people's pets!' Connie exclaimed.

'Yes, but I can't seem to prove that to him. If I could get hold of one of his traps and show him what he's doing to innocent pets, I'm sure he'd move the traps farther up the mountain. He's a reasonable man.'

Connie winced as she looked at the puppy's swollen paw. 'Mr. Aucker, Reggie hasn't been home for two days. Have you seen him?' she asked.

'He may be roaming. Tomcats do that, you know,' the vet said. 'By the way, Mrs. Aucker and I are looking forward to turkey with you and your mother tonight. Turkey's my favourite meal!'

'It's Reggie's too,' Connie said sadly. 'I just hope he isn't off in the woods in a trap somewhere.'

'Now that cat of yours is too smart to miss Christmas Eve dinner,' Mr. Aucker said, winking.

Connie helped in the kennels, then hurried home. Snow-flakes were falling thicker than ever. 'Here, Reggie!' she shouted again and again.

The afternoon seemed to last for ever even though Connie was busy. Finally she heard her mother's car enter the garage.

'Oh, Connie, the table looks so nice!' her mother exclaimed. 'That candle makes a pretty centrepiece. And the turkey smells done. Did you cook the potatoes?'

Connie nodded. 'They're almost ready.'

They were both busy working in the kitchen when the doorbell rang. 'I'll go,' Connie said.

'Mr. Aucker!' she exclaimed as she opened the door to her friend. 'I thought you weren't coming till six o'clock!'

He smiled broadly. 'I couldn't wait to give you a special Christmas present,' he said as he unwrapped the bundle in his arms.

'Reggie!' Connie shouted. 'Oh, Mr. Aucker, where did you find him?'

'I told you this rascal wouldn't miss out on turkey scraps,' he said. 'He even brought me a Christmas present.'

'A present?' Connie asked.

'Yes, this,' the doctor said, holding up a rusting chain with iron teeth attached. 'A trap! Your cat got caught, but he's made of strong stuff. He pulled the trap right out of the ground and managed to get back in time for feeding at the kennel. His leg is injured, but it will heal OK.'

Connie smiled tearfully as she took the cat in her arms. God had answered her prayer in His way. She had thought only of herself in asking for his return. God had answered her and would help others through Reggie.

'Reggie, you're not getting turkey scraps tonight,' she said. 'You're getting a whole drumstick!'

Reggie licked her cheek with his sandpaper tongue.

'And do I get the other drumstick?' Mr. Aucker asked.

'You certainly do,' Connie said, laughing. 'And a big thank-you hug as well!'

Casey, the Crow

A Nature Story by Delores Elaine Bius

SKINNY, BEDRAGGLED, and helpless, the baby crow would have made a tasty dinner for a cat. Fortunately, Roger Bius found the young bird and decided to raise him.

Roger, eleven, read all he could about crow care. He made Casey a cage to stay in at night. During the day, Casey could safely walk around in the fenced garden. (He couldn't fly because his wings hadn't developed yet.)

Like most young animals, Casey was always hungry. He had his mouth open, asking for food much of the time. At first, Roger was kept busy digging up worms. Later he fed Casey dog food, and then table scraps.

Mrs. Bius fed Casey while Roger was at school. When the crow was hungry he made an awful racket. It was impossible for Mrs. Bius to forget him. In fact, when Casey heard *anyone* coming to the back garden or opening the gate, he'd stop shrieking and run to the gate, expecting to be fed.

One day the postman asked Mrs. Bius, 'What kind of animal is in your garden? It makes a lot of noise.' When she showed him the young crow, he could hardly believe that such a small creature could make such a racket.

Casey enjoyed company. When Roger's father worked in the garage on his car, Casey would walk in and start chattering at him. Once, Casey went too close to an open can of oil. Afraid Casey would drink it, Mr. Bius shouted at him. Casey backed off as if he understood and went back into the garden.

Another time, Casey walked into the garage while Mr. Bius was working. The crow hopped up on to a box and watched as if inspecting everything Mr. Bius did.

Casey's favourite perch was on Roger's shoulder or hand. Casey also enjoyed bathing in the birdbath and having Roger gently towel him dry.

Crows are very intelligent birds. People who have studied them say they seem to think almost like people. They can even be taught to speak a few words.

Like other crows, Casey was attracted to bright objects.

He tried to peck at Mrs. Bius' watch and rings when she fed him. And he'd run around the garden, pecking at anything that caught his attention.

One time he found a box of metal washers. (A washer looks like a large coin with a hole in it.) Mr. Bius had left them in the garden.

When Roger came home from school, he found the washers stacked in the bottom of Casey's cage. Roger came into the house, laughing. 'Casey got a lot of exercise today,' he told his parents. 'He must have spent hours taking those washers one by one from the box to his cage.'

Casey was about two months old when Roger noticed that he wasn't growing properly. His feet and feathers seemed in good condition, but he flew only short distances.

Knowing that crows live in flocks, Roger thought Casey might be lonely and missing being with other birds. Roger's friend across the street had several birds and a larger garden, so Roger gave Casey to him.

Casey did much better after that. Though he never learned to fly far, he was more contented with other birds. And, of course, the Biuses were relieved to know he was getting along well.

Jesus once said, 'Consider the ravens [relatives of crows]: They do not sow or reap, they have no storeroom or barn; yet God feeds them. And how much more valuable you are than birds!' (Luke 12:24).

In Casey's situation, the Lord used Roger and his family to feed one of His birds.

The Camel

A Nature Story
by Grace Fox Anderson

GOD GAVE CAMELS perfect bodies for living in hot desert lands. They can go for days, in fact for weeks, without water—if they can eat juicy plants.

When in bad need of water, a camel can drink up to twenty-seven gallons in ten minutes! After a long drink, he will look swollen because the water goes right to his dry body tissues.

The camel's hump is a store of fat—extra energy for long journeys. His eyes are protected from wind-blown sand by long, thick eyelashes. Hair protects his ears. And he can close his nostrils when necessary.

His wide, two-toed feet do not bog down in desert sand.

They are padded on the bottom to protect them from hot sand.

Camel wool or hair makes a soft cloth. The hide or skin is used for water bags. Camels also provide meat and good milk.

They can be divided into two groups: pack camels and riding camels. Pack camels are used for carrying loads. They're the two-humped heavier animals. The one-humped Arabian camel is slimmer, more alert, and is used for riding.

Pack camels begin carrying loads at four years and can work till they are twenty-five or thirty years old. They may travel 100 miles a day across a desert with a load of 400 pounds! But they can carry up to 1,000 pounds for a short distance. They like to travel between two and four miles an hour, stopping to nibble at plants along the way.

Don't let the camel's silly 'smile' fool you. He is mean, stubborn, and untrustworthy. 'There are no wild camels and no tame ones,' is an old saying. Their slashing bite is twice as bad as a dog's. And they spit!

Yet maybe we'd be bad tempered too if we had to work in the hot desert sun, often with little food and water.

Our great Creator God certainly showed His sense of humour as well as wisdom when He made camels.

Brian and the Blind Cockerel

A Fiction Story by Delores Kading

BRIAN WOLKENS wasn't happy. It was early April, usually his favourite month because the winter snows had melted and he could play football again. Brian could score more goals than any other kid in Parkview School. But this year Brian knew he wouldn't be playing football for quite a while. He had fallen out of a tree the week before and had broken his leg.

'It's a simple fracture,' the doctor had told him, 'and you're young and strong, so you'll heal quickly. But you'll have to wear a cast on your leg at least six weeks.'

At first, it was kind of fun being the centre of attention with his cast. His classmates, teachers, and parents had autographed it. Some friends even drew funny pictures on it.

But in a few days, Brian was tired of being slow and clumsy. He knocked things over he didn't think he was near. And it was embarrassing to have the school bus driver get out and lift him into the bus because he couldn't swing the heavy cast up the high bus step. Besides, his leg hurt sometimes.

Brian began to feel very sorry for himself.

The worst thing, of course, was that he couldn't play football with his friends.

One day, his neighbour, Edwin, came up the driveway, carrying a box in his arms. Edwin was a young man with many hobbies. He also raised animals.

'Hi, Brian,' he said cheerfully. 'I hear you have some extra time on your hands this spring.'

Brian didn't want to be reminded. He didn't think anyone should be that cheerful either.

Edwin didn't seem to notice. 'I got my spring batch of young chickens a couple of weeks ago. One of the cockerels is blind. He finds the food and water OK, but the others push him away. They've already started picking on him. I don't have time to fuss over him, nor the room to keep him by himself. Would you like to raise him?'

Brian looked in the box. A scraggy, sorry-looking chicken

huddled in one corner with small white feathers sticking out of his yellow fuzz.

'This isn't the prettiest time of his life. He's just getting his feathers,' Edwin explained.

Animals had never interested Brian nearly as much as sports, but for some reason—maybe because the cockerel looked as unhappy as the boy felt—he nodded.

'Just keep his food and water in the same place so he can find them, and he'll get along fine,' Edwin told Brian. 'And have fun!'

Brian decided to call the cockerel 'Blindie' until he could think of a better name. But the name Blindie stuck.

Blindie soon had a home, complete with food and water, in the corner of the tool-shed. Brian sat on an old stool in the shed and watched the cockerel get used to his new home.

Blindie stood still for several minutes, then began to explore. The first thing he did was trip over his food trough and fall into it. He lay in the trough as if it was all part of his plan and immediately began to eat. He never tripped over the trough again.

Next, Blindie checked the size of his pen. He pecked here and there to get a feel of his surroundings.

'How do you like your new home, Blindie?' Brian asked. 'You won't have to worry about the other chickens being mean to you any more. And I'll be sure to keep food and water here for you.'

Brian hadn't talked much to animals. He was surprised to see how Blindie tilted his head to one side when Brian talked. Blindie was a good listener.

The young cockerel soon found a spot on the floor where the spring sun was shining in the window. He began to carefully preen and check his feathers. Finally, he put his head under his wing and went to sleep.

During school the next day, Brian thought about Blindie more than he thought about his schoolwork.

It was a sunny April day. When Brian finally got home from school, he carried Blindie outside to enjoy the new grass and warm air. Blindie got right to the business of scratching and pecking as if he could see exactly what he was doing.

That evening, as Brian was telling his mum and dad about having Blindie outside, he suddenly said, 'Help! I've just thought of something. If Blindie wanders off, he'll never find his way back again. He can't see which way to go.'

Brian found some old leather belts and fashioned a halter and lead out of them. From then on, Blindie wore his halter whenever he went outside. And he was tied to the clothesline so he couldn't wander off.

In the days and weeks that followed, Blindie feathered out into an attractive young cockerel. He experimented with crowing, first as a croaky yip that surprised even himself. Finally he graduated to a full-throated, loud, wing-flapping 'cock-a-doodle-do!' And he ran towards the sound of Brian's voice whenever the boy talked to him.

One evening as Brian sat in the shed watching Blindie, the animal kept arching his neck over the bottom rung of the ladder stored there. He tried to get first one leg, then the other up to the bottom step, but he couldn't quite reach it. He wanted a perch to sleep on, as all birds do. When Brian realized what Blindie was trying to do, he set him on the step. The cockerel fluffed his feathers, and tilted his head at Brian.

'You're saying "thank you," aren't you, you silly cockerel. Go to sleep.'

Blindie did.

Sometimes winter likes to have a last fling even though the calendar has been saying it's April for almost four weeks.

Brian sat in school watching the wet slushy snow cover the new green grass and flowers. After school, his mum picked him up and took him to the doctor for a checkup.

'Your leg seems to be coming along fine, Brian,' the doctor said, smiling. 'We can take the cast off in another ten days. You may even be playing football before the summer is over.'

'Great!' Brian beamed. Then he looked a little sheepish and admitted, 'I guess I'm getting along with my cast better now than I did at first. But I'll still be glad to get it off!'

The snow was still falling and a chilly wind whined around the car as Brian and Mrs. Wolkens turned into their driveway.

'Mum, the tool-shed door is open! The wind must have blown it open. If only Blindie had sense enough to stay inside.'

But the tool-shed was empty. Blindie was gone.

'I'll help you look,' Brian's mother offered. 'I'll go one way and you go the other.'

'OK, Mum, but look fast. Blindie might have frozen to death.'

Brian had told his mother to hurry, but he found that he could hardly walk himself. The snow was several inches deep and very wet and slippery. His cast had never been such a burden, and he was in such a hurry.

'Blindie! Blindie!' he kept calling, hoping the cockerel would come to the sound of his voice.

Sweat was trickling down Brian's back in spite of the freezing temperature and icy wind. He gasped for breath, but still called, 'Blindie! Blindie!' If Blindie wasn't found before dark, the boy knew the little cockerel would not live through the night.

Brian was on Edwin's property now. He wondered if

Blindie could have gone this far. Maybe he should turn back and try another direction.

Suddenly Brian fell headfirst into the snow. He had tripped over a low fence that Edwin used for his baby ducks. Brian had known the fence was there, but his cast just hadn't cleared the top as he thought it would.

It felt so good to lie down and rest that Brian didn't move for a few minutes. Then he noticed a mound of snow lying against the fence just a few inches from his face. Was it his imagination or was it moving slightly?

'Blindie?' he asked softly. Immediately the snow mound began to stir, then to flap, and there was Blindie struggling to his feet.

Brian got up, brushed off the half-frozen cockerel, and cradled him in his arms. 'You must have done the same thing I did, Blindie. Tripped on the fence and stayed there to rest. Except you got covered with snow. Let's go home.'

He wrapped Blindie in a warm towel and carefully placed him in a box in the kitchen. The poor cockerel still shivered, and sometimes his head bobbed as he dozed off to sleep.

Before Brian went to bed, he sat down by the box.

'You know, Blindie, this cast I'm wearing saved your life. If I hadn't been wearing it, I probably wouldn't have tripped on that old fence. And if I hadn't fallen right there, I probably never would have seen you. It was a close call.'

Blindie shivered in agreement. Then he lifted his head high and tilted it in Brian's direction.

Brian answered, 'You're welcome.'

The Trouble with George

A Fiction Story by Gwen Pierce-Jones

'MUM, I'M GOING NOW,' shouted ten-year-old David Kent as he bounced his bike down the steps from the back door. Pokey, his Beagle puppy, scurried under his feet, hoping he could go along.

David gently pushed the puppy back inside. 'You can't go to school, Pokey,' David said.

A mellow 'honk! honk!' broke the morning stillness. Streaming across the sky were two dotted lines, forming a wavy letter V.

David opened the kitchen door and called inside, 'Mum! The Canada geese are flying south. Come outside.'

The geese flew lower as they approached the Kent home. David could see their black heads, necks outstretched, and grey bodies.

'A sure sign of winter,' Mrs. Kent said as she stood in the doorway, holding Pokey.

David pointed to the cornfield that met the Kent's property line. 'It looks as if they're heading for Mr. Miller's place.'

The Kents had moved to their small home last spring.

The housing development where they lived was new, but there were still quite a few old farms in the area.

As the birds slowly descended, a shot rang out! In frantic confusion, the birds flew in all directions. All except one. It fell into the golden cornstalks.

David raced into the field.

'Come back!' cried Mrs. Kent.

Wildly he crashed through the field, not really knowing whether he was looking for the hunter or the goose. He stopped suddenly. The injured goose was lying right in front of him, trying desperately to look like a rock.

'Now, now, don't be afraid,' David spoke softly. His stomach turned when he saw a dark-red splotch of blood on the feathers.

'Hiss!' The bird had a look of terror and lunged at David when he approached.

David remembered a sandwich he had stashed in his pocket. 'Here, fellow,' he said softly as he threw a piece to the bird. 'I won't hurt you.'

The bird swallowed the bread and began to settle down.

'I must get you out of here,' said David. 'But how?'

He thought of his jacket. Quickly he took it off. Then he pulled up two cornstalks and shoved them through the sleeves. After placing the goose on the jacket he pulled it along the rows of corn, using the stalks as handles.

When David reached the garden, his mother and father both ran to help.

'Where's Pokey? Don't let him out!'

'He's in the house,' Mrs. Kent answered. 'But that goose is hurt, David. What are you going to do?'

'I'm going to try to save him, Mum,' he answered. 'I couldn't leave him there!'

'Let me have a look at him,' Mr. Kent said. But as the tall man approached, the goose hissed again.

'Here, Dad, give him something to eat,' David suggested. 'He wasn't as scared of me after I gave him some bread.'

After a careful check, Mr. Kent stood up. 'You know,' he said with a grin, 'I think he'll be OK. It seems that the shot only grazed his flesh and a few feathers.'

'Can I keep him?' David asked.

'Only until he's better,' Mother said. 'God didn't put wild creatures on earth to be penned up.'

'Let's put him in the garage,' Mr. Kent suggested. 'David, you can pick up some hay on your way home from school.'

That evening at the dinner table, David talked of nothing but the goose. 'I even found out what geese eat,' he announced. 'They like corn and grain, and in the spring they eat new shoots. They also have to have a little gravel to digest their food.'

'David, don't get too attached to that goose,' his father reminded. 'You must let him go as soon as he is better.'

'I think I'll call him George. That's a nice name for a Canadian goose. What do you think, Mum?'

'I don't think you should give him a name,' she answered.

David was so excited he didn't really hear his parents' remarks. 'Now we have to decide where to keep him,' he said.

His parents looked at each other and shook their heads. 'What's the use?' said Mr. Kent. 'Why don't we build him a pen next to the garage? We'll keep him there until he's well.'

By the next evening the pen was built, and after a few weeks everyone, except Pokey, had grown fond of George. George had a bad habit of gently nipping Pokey on the backside. The poor puppy would start to howl and head for the house. This went on for several weeks until one day the small dog turned around and growled at the big bird.

'Look!' cried David. 'Pokey finally stood his ground.'

From that time on the big goose and the growing puppy became friends.

It was early December. David's father brought up the subject of George at the dinner table. 'You should let him go,' said Mr. Kent. 'George is a wild bird. He wasn't meant to be penned up.'

'I know, Dad,' David said. 'But it's getting colder every day. He isn't as strong as he was. He hasn't even tried out his wings.'

'I know, but—'

Tap. Tap. Someone knocking on the back door interrupted Mr. Kent.

David opened the door. His heart dropped when he saw it was Mr. Miller, the farmer who owned the cornfield next to them.

'David!' He spoke sharply. 'May I have a talk with your parents about that goose?' He pointed to the pen. Pokey jumped at the man's trousers and playfully pulled on his cuff.

He jerked his leg away. 'And I would like to talk about that dog too!'

'Well, good evening, Mr. Miller,' Mrs. Kent said pleasantly when the farmer entered the warm kitchen. 'What brings you out on such a cold evening?'

Mr. Miller got right to the point. 'Do you know that your son allows that goose and dog to roam all over the countryside?' he asked. His face was red. 'This afternoon they were over in my farmyard chasing my chickens. And they scared my daughter Beth out of her wits. That goose bit her!'

'He does that sometimes,' David said. 'But he's only playing.' David felt he had to defend George.

74

'Well, my Beth didn't think he was playing!' shouted Mr. Miller. 'Not only do you city people move in and build on perfectly good farmland. You allow your children and pets to roam all over everyone's property.'

'Now, Mr. Miller,' Mr. Kent interrupted. 'I know you must be upset because the farm next to yours was sold for housing. But my family only bought what was already built. However, you have every right to be upset about George and Pokey.' He turned to David. 'I told you not to let them leave our garden!'

'I'm sorry,' David said. 'But I was riding my bike and they followed me. You know how they always do. Then they just took off. By the time I could get them, the damage was done.'

'You know you're keeping a wild bird, don't you?' Mr. Miller said. 'Wild birds can be shot. The next time I see that goose, he'll be on my dinner table.'

'Now, Mr. Miller,' Mr. Kent said. 'What would that solve? The goose will be gone in the spring. Until then we'll keep a close watch on him.' He turned to David. 'Won't we, Son?'

'Yes, Father!' David answered quickly. His dad did say spring, didn't he?

'And watch that dog too!' Mr. Miller said as he headed for the door.

'Well!' Mrs. Kent exclaimed when Mr. Miller left. 'He didn't even say "Good evening"!'

David was upset. 'He probably was the one who shot George in the first place. And he has a *No Hunting* sign on his farm. No hunting for everyone but him.'

'Now, David, you can't accuse Mr. Miller of shooting George. And you can't blame him for being angry. Those two must have caused quite a rumpus this afternoon.' And Mr. Kent began to chuckle. David joined him, imagining the scene.

Mrs. Kent smiled and then became serious. 'Mr. Miller is right about one thing, David. George is a wild bird. As soon as spring comes, you must let him go.'

Things went fine for David over the winter. He made new friends in school and joined a Bible club at the new church. The months passed quickly. By early March, the snow had begun to melt and crocuses were beginning to poke up in the flower beds around the house.

David was doing his homework one evening when his mother brought up the subject of George: 'I noticed Mr. Miller is beginning to plant,' she said. 'You know geese love fresh young shoots, David. You must keep a close watch on George.'

'He can't get out of his pen,' David said.

'That's another thing,' Mrs. Kent added. 'Don't you think you're being unfair? George is wild. He doesn't want to be penned up for the rest of his life.'

'He won't go,' said David. 'He likes it here.'

'You're not being fair,' Mrs. Kent answered.

The next morning as David was about to deliver his newspapers, he saw Mr. Miller coming across the lawn.

'David!' he shouted. 'Your goose is in my field. I'll give you one minute to get him out. Then I'm going for my gun.'

David raced across the lawn and into the field. 'George!' he cried.

The goose looked up and slowly waddled towards him.

'I'm sorry, Mr. Miller,' David said as he pushed him into the pen, 'but somehow he opened the latch.'

'You should let that goose go, young man!' scolded Mr. Miller.

'He won't go!' David cried.

'He'll go. When the geese fly north again, he'll go.'

That evening at the dinner table David told his father about Mr. Miller's visit. 'I'm going to put a padlock on the pen,' he said. 'That goose is getting too clever.'

'David, Mr. Miller is right. George should be free.'

'He won't go!' David cried. 'He hasn't tried to fly even once.'

'He hasn't tried to fly because he had no reason to, Son,' Mr. Kent said.

'I won't let him go!' said David. 'He'll die! He won't be able to take care of himself.'

That night when David prayed he asked God for guidance. Was he being fair? He knew from the beginning that he didn't want to give up the goose. His parents were always saying, 'The trouble with George is he's wild.' The real trouble with George, David felt, was that he was a pet. He needed protection, but nobody else saw it that way.

The next day in school David had a hard time thinking.

'My first question, class,' began his history teacher, 'is: If you had been an American Indian when the white man started West, what would you have done?'

'I would have fought,' Bill said. 'The white man took away their land.'

David thought of Mr. Miller. He was fighting too—trying to protect his land and crops.

'But they had treaties,' Jan said.

'The treaties were broken,' David put in. 'They put the Indians on reservations.'

'That must have been the worst,' Bill said. 'You know, the Indians were free to roam the country, but they had both their land and freedom taken away.'

That evening when David got off the school bus, he heard honking in the distance. The geese were flying north. He knew what he had to do. He had received the answer to his prayer while they were talking in school about the Indians' freedom being taken away. He ran to George's pen and opened the door. Tears brimmed in his eyes when he let the goose waddle out.

'Shoo! Shoo!' he cried.

'Uh-wonk! Uh-wonk!' George answered the flying geese. He spread his powerful wings and with a few rapid strokes he was airborne.

'Good-bye, George!' David cried. 'Take care of yourself!' With tears streaming down his face, he ran into the house and up to his bedroom. Sometimes doing the right thing really hurt.

'I'm proud of you, Son,' said Mr. Kent that evening. 'That was a hard thing to do.'

'Please, Dad,' said David. 'I would rather not talk about it.'

The months passed and the hurt David felt every time someone mentioned George began to fade. When the family laughed about the funny things George did, David laughed too.

Then it was autumn again. Several times David heard flocks of geese overhead as they made their way to the southern feeding grounds.

'Do you think George is with that flock?' asked David one day as a mellow *Honk! Honk!* filled the morning air.

David dropped his spoon. 'Hey, listen! There's one in the garden!' He raced to the door and saw a big grey goose standing in the garden.

'Quick, Mum,' he cried. 'Give me some bread.'

As David ran down the steps, Pokey dashed past him and raced out to meet the unexpected guest. The goose waddled towards them. David flung his arms around the grey body, and the goose gently laid his black head on the boy's shoulder.

'It's him!' cried David. 'It's George!'

His parents were standing in the doorway.

'Don't worry, Dad!' he shouted. 'He's only here for a visit.'

George spent a few hours with the Kents. Then he spread his wings and flew off to join his flock.

'I'm really glad he stopped here,' David said as George disappeared into the distance. 'Now I know he's OK. And he knows I'm OK. And do you know what?'

'No, what?' asked Mrs. Kent as she wiped a tear from her eye.

'I'll bet he stops again on his way north when spring comes!'

Bashful Runner

by Gloria A. Truitt

It's hard to spot me in the woods
   When I'm among the trees,
For God gave me a camouflage
   To fool my enemies.
I'm noted for my big, sad eyes.
   I'm gentle as can be!
My food of berries, leaves, and grass
   Is *yummy-yum* to me!
The Bible tells you I am swift.
   In a *flash* I'll disappear,
Bounding through the forest brush
   For I'm a bashful deer!
(Song of Solomon 2:8–9)

Mule Sense

Told by Anna C. Atwood
Written by Grace Fox

MRS. ANNA ATWOOD OF THE CENTRAL AMERICAN MISSION HAS BEEN ON A MULEBACK EVANGELISTIC TRIP IN THE HONDURAS MOUNTAINS. SHE HAS TWO COMPANIONS. ONE IS 81-YEAR-OLD DON MODESTO RODRIGUEZ, A LAY PREACHER. THE OTHER IS ARBELIA ARDON.

THE MULES ARE A NUISANCE! ONE BOLTS FOR HOME. IT TAKES DON MODESTO HOURS TO BRING HIM BACK. NOW AS THEY TRAVEL HOME TO DULCE NOMBRE DE COPAN, MRS. ATWOOD'S MULE LEAVES THE GROUP...

... AND WALKS INTO THE GARDEN OF A MOUNTAIN HOME.

ANYONE HERE?

WHEN NO ONE ANSWERS AT THE FIRST HOUSE, SHE GOES NEXT DOOR AND OFFERS THEM A TRACT.

NO ONE HERE READS, BUT OUR NEIGHBOURS DO. TAKE IT TO THEM.

Where Is Snow?

A Fiction Story by Gloria A. Truitt

Though the people in this story are not real, the white deer at the zoo in Marquette, Michigan, USA, is quite real.

THE EDITOR

EARLY ONE SPRING MORNING, Mr. Olson was walking through the pine-scented woods along the south shore of Lake Superior near Marquette, Michigan. He worked for the Department of Natural Resources, and he was looking for animals that had been weakened by the long winter.

Pushing his way through the undergrowth, he caught sight of a small mound of snow. 'That's strange,' he said to himself. 'All the other snow has melted. I wonder why that hasn't?'

He was about to walk past when the 'snow' moved. Curious, he stepped closer and stared into two pink eyes above a small pink nose.

It was a fawn, but the strangest Mr. Olson had ever seen. Instead of a speckled brown, the fawn was completely white, except for its pink eyes and nose.

He leaned over and saw that it was injured. And it had sores on its face and body. 'Well, fellow, you look about a year old. But I can see you're too weak to stand on those spindly legs,' Mr. Olson said kindly.

He gently picked up the animal and carried it to his truck. He knew the deer could never survive by itself in the cold; and he knew exactly where he would take it. Marquette had a zoo with a lovely deer park. There, the albino fawn would be nursed back to health and given a safe home.

The townspeople quickly learned of the new addition to their zoo. They came by the dozens to peer through the wire fence at the unusual creature Mr. Olson named Snow.

Most of the deer came to the fence to nibble offerings of carrots and lettuce. But poor Snow stood at a distance, watching nervously from his own separate pen.

One day Mr. Olson pulled up in his truck. Beside him sat his ten-year-old daughter, Beth. 'Oh, Daddy,' she said, 'we forgot the carrots!'

'No, we didn't, Beth,' her father said as he tossed a small paper bag full of carrots into her lap. They walked up to the fence and, sure enough, several deer hurried to push their noses through the wire openings.

'Where is Snow?' Beth asked. 'I don't see him anywhere.'

'Look over there,' her father directed. 'He's in his own pen in the far corner where he won't be hurt by the other deer.'

'What do you mean?' Beth asked. 'Why would the others hurt him?'

'Because he's different.'

Tears gathered in Beth's eyes. 'Oh, I wish animals were like people and could understand Jesus' command about loving each other. Just think how happy Snow would be!'

'That's true,' Mr. Olson said. 'But sometimes people also reject others who are new or different.'

As Beth stared at the lonely white deer, she thought suddenly of her forthcoming birthday party. She had invited all the girls around her home—but one.

Beth tugged at her father's sleeve. 'Let's hurry, Daddy,' she said. 'I've just remembered something I have to take care of at home.'

Rushing into the house, Beth grabbed a blank invitation to her birthday party. She quickly printed in the time and date of the party. Then she ran across the street and knocked at the door where new neighbours had moved in the week before.

When she knocked, a girl about her own age answered.

'Hi!' Beth said. 'You're Vickie, aren't you? I know you've just moved here, but I'd like you to come to my birthday party on Saturday. I'm Beth and I live across the street.'

'I'd love to come!' Vickie said, smiling. 'Mother!' she called over her shoulder. 'Mother, I've just met my first friend in Marquette!'

As she walked back home, Beth prayed silently, 'Thank you, Jesus, for reminding me that we should "love one another". Please forgive me for almost leaving Vickie out just because she's new.'

Several months later, Mr. Olson drove Beth to the zoo again. Beth ran to the fence where the deer lived. In her hand was a bunch of carrots. She looked across to the far corner, but no Snow! 'Oh, Daddy, where is Snow? I hope nothing's happened to him.'

Mr. Olson put his arm around her and pointed to the herd of brown deer coming towards them. Walking contentedly with the herd was Snow!

'I wanted to surprise you,' he said, chuckling. 'See? Even deer can learn to "love one another"!'

Beth laughed as the animals pushed their noses through the openings of the fence. Guess which one got the first carrot?

The Return of Midnight

A Fiction Story by Craig Massey

'JUST THINK, TODD, by this time tomorrow, David will be here to take Midnight back to Mexico,' Tammy said.

Tammy Taylor was talking to her twin brother as they sat on the porch of their rambling white ranch house in Colorado, USA, playing a game.

'It's been six months since he wrote about needing a horse. Those mountains must be pretty rugged if he can't get around in a jeep,' Todd added, watching a herd of shorthorn cattle grazing in the fields beyond their house.

'I'm going to miss Midnight,' Tammy said, with a trace of sadness.

'I guess I will too, but don't forget, Sis, that's why we got him in the first place. David needs a big, strong horse that will be able to carry him and his packs to those hard-to-reach villages.'

'I know Midnight will be good on rocky trails,' Tammy replied. 'He's as sure-footed as a mountain goat. And just think, he will be helping David take the gospel to people who have never heard of Jesus.'

The moment the twelve-year-old twins had heard that their older, missionary brother needed a horse, they had decided to see what they could do. They had asked Dad, but he had said there was no horse on the ranch that would be suitable for mountain work. So right then, they had begun to pray for a horse. And within a month the answer had come from an unexpected source.

It had happened when they were leaving church one Sunday morning. Mr. Foxx, a neighbouring rancher, had approached them and asked, 'Is it true that you're looking for a horse for David?'

'Yes!' the twins had said together.

'Well, yesterday I rounded up about forty wild horses to ship east,' Mr. Foxx had said. 'There are several beauties in the lot. You can come over tomorrow and take your pick. I'd like to help David in his ministry too.'

The next day Todd and Tammy had gone with their father and picked out the finest horse in the lot. They had promptly named him Midnight because of his shiny black coat.

For the first few weeks the wild horse had seemed afraid of everything, but the twins had treated him kindly. Todd had taught him to come when he whistled. Both twins had carried sugar or carrots in their pockets. When Midnight obeyed, he always got something as a reward.

Now Midnight was friendly and obedient. And David was due home to pick him up.

As Todd waited for Tammy to take her turn at the game, he noticed a lone rider approaching in a cloud of dust. 'Looks like someone in a big hurry!' he exclaimed.

They jumped up from the steps where they were sitting and ran together to meet the galloping rider. 'That's Sleepy,'

Tammy said. 'He'd never ride fast unless something was really wrong!'

Just then Sleepy reined up in a cloud of yellow dust. The old bewhiskered cowboy, who worked for their father, slid from the saddle. 'Got bad news, kids!' he said. 'I've just been down to the field where the horses usually graze. Midnight ain't there. I scouted all over, but not a trace.'

'Did he break through the fence?' Tammy asked.

'Don't rightly know. I couldn't find any breaks. Besides, the other horses are all still there. I reckon somebody's taken that horse.'

'I can't believe it!' Tammy cried. 'Who would do that? And what will we tell David? He's supposed to be home tomorrow.'

'Listen, Tammy,' Todd said. 'You go and tell Dad what's happened. I'm going to saddle up Star and see if I can find any signs of Midnight.' And before Tammy could answer, Todd was running towards the corral.

He called to Star and soon had his brown pony heading for the south end of the ranch where the younger horses were kept.

Who would steal Midnight, Todd wondered. *Maybe Sleepy was wrong. But then how could the horse escape on his own?*

When Todd reached the field, he glanced over the herd and saw right away that Midnight was gone. *Maybe someone just opened the gate, took him out, and rode off on him,* Todd thought. *I'll ride towards canyon country. That's where a thief would likely try to hide.*

The sun began dropping in the western skies, casting deep purple shadows on the mountains. In the quiet, afternoon heat, Todd prayed earnestly that the Lord would help him find their horse.

He scanned the countryside for two hours but saw no sign of Midnight. Discouraged, he headed back to the ranch to see if something had turned up. It was then that he spotted movement far ahead of him near a small wood.

Todd took his field glasses from his saddlebag and focused on the moving objects. A lone rider was leading five horses and one of them was jet black—like Midnight!

'Wh-why, it's—at least it looks like—Midnight!' he exclaimed. 'Now if I can only catch him before he gets behind those trees. Once he passes there, he'll be in the canyons. With the thousands of hiding places there, I'll never find them.'

Todd spurred his pony to a ground-eating canter. Several times he took out the glasses, but the horses were too far away to tell for sure if the black one was Midnight. The rider did not seem to know he was being followed, for he kept up a slow pace.

When the sun slid behind the mountains, Todd realized his chances of catching up with the horses and rider were slim. The strange rider had almost reached the trees. Todd urged Star to greater speed, but it was too late. The horses and rider had disappeared into the wood.

Disappointed, Todd slowed down but kept on towards the wood, praying that he might yet find Midnight.

Twilight had settled when he entered the wood. He stopped and listened. At first he heard nothing; then came the sound of muffled hoofbeats. He couldn't tell whether they were coming or going. He waited a few minutes before realizing that the rider was coming straight at him.

His heart beat faster and cold sweat broke out on his forehead. What would he do if he came face to face with the thief? Would he be able to persuade him to give Midnight back? Again Todd prayed for help.

Just then a man broke through the trees, riding towards Todd without the other horses. Todd felt weak with relief when he recognized the man—Mr. Evans, a trusted fellow rancher who lived about four miles from the Taylor ranch.

'What are you doing way out here at dusk, Todd?' Mr. Evans asked, reining up his horse beside Todd.

'The horse that we were going to give my missionary brother is missing,' Todd answered.

'Do you mean someone stole it?' Mr. Evans asked.

'Well, I don't know, but it could be. Midnight's not in the field.'

'Oh, so that's why you followed me,' Mr. Evans said, chuckling. 'You thought I was the horse thief.'

'You were so far away, I couldn't see who you were. But I saw a black horse and thought it looked like Midnight,' Todd explained.

'Well, Todd, I'm sorry about your missing horse, but the black one you saw is mine. I just put him and the others out to range. C'mon, ride through the wood with me. Perhaps you can still see him.'

Todd rode beside Mr. Evans until they came to the clearing. Mr. Evans pointed to the horses, and even in the fading light, Todd could see that the black horse was nothing at all like Midnight. Feeling a little foolish, he said, 'Thanks, Mr. Evans. I can see he isn't our horse.'

'Well, Todd, I have to move along—you'd better too. It will be dark in a few minutes. If I see any sign of your horse, I'll phone when I get home,' he called back over his shoulder.

Todd took a narrow trail that led into undergrowth, thinking it would be quicker than returning through the wood. He hoped to make it at least halfway home before dark, and urged Star into a fast trot.

But while moving along at that pace, Star suddenly shied,

twisting so sharply he sent Todd flying through the air. At the same moment, Todd saw a huge diamondback rattlesnake on the trail.

Todd hit the ground with a thud and his horse galloped off in fright. How long Todd lay unconscious he did not know, but the blackness all around him when he slowly opened his eyes made him realize it had been some time. Stabbing pains ripped through his body. His head hurt and his ankle throbbed.

Dazed, he tried to recall what had happened. Gradually, he remembered the snake on the trail and feared that it might have bitten his leg, causing the awful pain. He tried to sit up, but a warning rattle froze him. The snake was still nearby— only a few feet from his head.

'God, please help me!' he cried out.

A slight sound caught his ear—the sound of the snake sliding through dry grass at the edge of the trail. It came

nearer and nearer. He could not see in the darkness, but suddenly he felt the snake's cold body slither over his arm. Breathless, he waited, expecting any moment to feel the fangs sink into his flesh.

Slowly the sinuous body slid off and into the undergrowth. Only when the rustling in the grass had faded did Todd breathe normally again. He raised himself up and felt his ankle. It seemed twice its natural size. He realized now that he must have twisted it when he fell off the horse.

Todd tried to stand, hoping to get home, but his leg would not hold him. However, he felt no panic now. If the Lord could keep that rattler from biting him, he reasoned, surely He could keep Todd safe for the rest of the night.

Some hours later, morning broke in the east, revealing black storm clouds rolling in from the southeast. Todd managed to hobble to his feet and find a stick to use as a crutch.

With great pain, he worked his way down the trail until he came to a bubbling spring. The cool, clear water satisfied his thirst. As he knelt there, a slight noise caused him to glance up.

To his amazement, he saw a wild horse step from the undergrowth, then another, and a third. The third horse was jet-black and Todd almost cried out in surprise when he recognized Midnight!

With a prayer on his lips, he whistled softly to the horse. The instant the others heard it, they bolted. But Midnight paused and looked towards Todd. The second whistle brought the horse to a stop.

Todd felt in his pocket and found a lump of sugar still intact. Midnight saw the motion and sniffed the air. Slowly, he turned and walked towards Todd's outstretched hand.

Todd got carefully to his feet. He didn't want to stumble and scare off the horse. Midnight seemed to be arguing with himself: *Should I go with my wild friends or should I return to this boy who always treated me kindly?*

The sugar tempted Midnight and he came within a few feet of Todd, who drew back his hand, hoping to lure the horse close enough so he could grasp the leather halter still on his head.

As Midnight stepped closer and took the sugar, Todd carefully reached up for the halter and grasped it firmly, talking quietly to Midnight. With great effort, Todd managed to pull himself up on Midnight's back. His ankle ached fiercely but his joy in finding the horse helped.

'Thanks, Lord Jesus!' Todd breathed as he leaned over and patted Midnight's smooth black coat and headed him towards the ranch. 'Good boy, Midnight. You'll never know how glad I am to find you,' he said. 'Now let's get home before the rain comes.'

They were about halfway home when big drops of water

began to splatter the dry ground and rocks around horse and rider. Todd headed for an abandoned cabin to wait for the storm to pass. He couldn't risk Midnight bolting again.

By the time he reached the shelter, deep rumbling thunder rolled overhead and lightning zigzagged across the sky.

Todd slipped off Midnight in front of the cabin door and hobbled in, leading Midnight inside after him. It was so dark he didn't notice the man standing in the shadows.

Todd stood in the doorway, holding Midnight and watching the torrent of rain splatter the earth. From behind him, a deep voice caused Todd to whirl around so quickly that his ankle sent fiery pain through his body and he gasped.

'Why don't you tie your horse in the shed behind the cabin and come inside?'

Something about the voice seemed familiar to Todd and he called, 'Who's there?'

'Say, is that you, Todd?' the man asked in return.

In a flash Todd recognized the man as he moved into the light of the doorway. 'David!' he cried.

'I didn't know you at first, Todd,' David said, as he hugged his younger brother. 'You've grown really tall!'

'Wow! Am I glad to see you, David,' Todd cried. 'When did you get home? How did you get here?'

David put up his hand and laughed. 'Hold on. Give me a chance. I got in last night and found that both you and the horse were missing. We hunted all night for you.'

He patted the horse at Todd's side. 'This must be Midnight,' he said. 'How did you find him?'

While the two brothers waited for the rain to stop, Todd told his story. He finished by saying, 'The one thing that still puzzles me is how Midnight got out of the field.'

David laughed. 'Dad studied the ground around the fenced-off section of the corral last night and found where several wild horses had come around. Evidently, Midnight broke through a weak place in the fence.'

'Well, I'm glad to know that no one stole him,' Todd said.

'And I'm glad to find you both alive and not too badly off after your adventure,' David said. 'Mum and Dad are pretty worried about you—not to mention Tammy.'

'Now that it's brightening up outside, let me look at that ankle. I've even had to do a little medical work in Mexico. No doctors in those mountain villages, you know. Midnight will be a big help in getting me around, thanks to you and Tammy.'

How to Wake Up a Dormouse

A Nature Story by Grace Helen Davis

DORMICE ARE some of the prettier members of the mouse family. They have big eyes, long feathery tails, and big furry ears. The back of the dormouse is reddish brown. Its stomach is creamy white.

The hazel dormouse has a three-inch tail and three-inch body. It nests in leaves at the base of a tree or in bushes, usually in the woods. It looks and acts like a tiny squirrel.

Dormice sit up to eat the way squirrels, gerbils, and hamsters do, holding bits of food in their tiny paws. They eat seeds, fruit, insects, eggs, grain, and nuts.

They are common in Europe and Asia Minor. The hazel dormouse used to be kept as a pet by children in southern England. But it is no longer common here. The grey squirrel has taken over its nests.

The 'dor' in dormouse means sleep. The dormouse is a lively little animal in the summer-time. But the moment the weather turns cold, he hibernates. That means he goes to sleep for the winter.

In fact, a dormouse sometimes hides away and sleeps during a cool spell in the summer. As soon as it warms up, the dormouse wakes up. When a pet dormouse is asleep or hibernating, it can't be awakened by shouting or even by being rolled around. Can you guess how it can be awakened?

All its owner needs to do is hold his tiny pet in his warm hands. Presto! A cute ear will lift or a tiny paw will stretch out. Soon the dormouse unfolds and is dashing about or asking for something to eat. Only warmth will wake him up.

Maybe you have a 'dormouse' at home—a younger brother or sister who never listens to you. You tease him, shout at him, and beg him, but he won't respond.

Try being kind to him. You'll find that his love for you will wake right up. He'll want to please you and will be glad to do as you ask.

The warmth of kindness goes farther than anything else with little children—with bigger ones and grown-ups too. Is it any wonder that God said, 'Be kind and compassionate to one another, forgiving each other' (Ephesians 4:32).

Up, Up, and Away!

A True Story by Grace Fox Anderson

IF YOU'VE EVER been handed a helium-filled balloon only to have it slip from your hand and soar off into outer space, you know kind of how I felt that evening.

I was washing up supper dishes with Peeper, my mother's green and yellow parakeet on my shoulder. He was bobbing up and down, talking, and whistling in my ear as I worked. I picked up the rubbish bag, stepped out the back door of our small house, and dropped the bag into the dustbin.

Startled by the sudden *clunk* of the bag landing in the bin, Peeper soared off into the sky, while I stood there feeling as helpless and hopeless as if I'd lost a helium balloon—only much worse. Peeper had been our pet for five years—ever since we kids had given him to Mother, to keep her company after Daddy died.

'Mum,' I called into the house, 'Peeper has flown off. I'm going after him.'

I turned and ran in the direction I'd seen him take—across our neighbour's garden and the garden behind it. Mum, about sixty-five then, came trotting along behind me. We called and listened. Finally we heard the shrill whistles

only a parakeet can make—right above our heads in a tall elm tree.

'Peeper, come down,' we coaxed. 'Peeper; Peeper, come to us. Come, pretty bird.' We said all the things you say to try to coax a frightened pet to come; but Peeper seemed to be having a great time—running up and down a large branch, showing off for his growing audience.

Several neighbours' children gathered around us and we explained what had happened. They were very sympathetic. One boy even said he'd climb the tree except it was too wide and tall.

We spent a lot of time there, trying to think of some way to get Peeper to fly down to us, but nothing worked. Finally we thought of getting his cage, and I hurried home for it. But when I got back, he was gone.

'As soon as you left, he flew off after you,' Mother said.

We carried his cage in the direction Peeper had flown, but it was getting dark. We couldn't see him and couldn't even hear him this time, though we walked quite a distance.

What had become of our little bird? Moreover, what *would* become of our little bird? True, it was summer-time. But would he know where to get food or water? Would other birds or some cat or dog get him?

Back home, we sat down wearily at our kitchen table. 'I can't tell you how awful I feel,' I said. 'I simply didn't remember he was on my shoulder when I stepped out the back door. When he flew off, I was as startled as he was.'

Mother didn't lecture me. We had both received Jesus as Saviour long before that. We looked to Him for every need. We had gone through some rough times since Daddy died, but our Lord had never deserted us. Now we decided to take this problem to the Lord too.

'Father, our little bird means a lot to us,' Mother prayed. 'We've had him for five years now. He isn't used to flying free. He won't know where to get food or how to find us. Please, somehow help us *find* him.'

The next day, Saturday, we drove around in the car looking for Peeper. But how would we find a small green bird among all the green trees and bushes and lawns in our big city? Well, we simply didn't.

On Sunday we went to church as usual, and I taught my Sunday school class of ten-year-old girls. They prayed with me for Peeper. Monday was a holiday—not a very happy one. Still no sign of Peeper. On Tuesday, I thought about our little bird while I was at work—and prayed for him.

When I got home that day, Mother said, 'I had an idea today. I was listening to our local radio station. They have a programme where people call in about pets. I phoned and told them about Peeper, so they took our telephone number.'

'Mum, that's great!' I exclaimed, feeling a surge of new hope. 'I know you don't usually listen to that station. God must have led you to listen to that programme today.'

The next afternoon at work, I got a hurry-up call from Mother just before going-home time. 'If you can come home now, please do,' she said. 'A lady just phoned and thinks she may have Peeper.'

I left work and ran most of the half mile home. We

grabbed Peeper's cage and jumped into the car. As I drove, Mum told me about the phone call and where the lady lived.

'She said she found the parakeet out on her dustbin. I told her to stoop down so he'd jump on her shoulder.'

When she reached the lady's house—just a mile from us— she came out and told us she had the bird in her garage. 'I did just as you said,' she told Mother.

'It must be Peeper,' I said. But when I saw him, I wasn't so certain. Surely this bedraggled little creature with drooping wings and closed eyes, sitting on the back of a chair, wasn't our bright-eyed, lively little bird.

Mum went carefully up to him. 'Peeper, hop in your cage,' she said as she held the cage beside him. But he didn't move; so she gently picked him up and put him in. 'He looks half dead and probably is,' Mother said. 'After all, he's been gone five days. It's a miracle that we've found him.'

We stayed a little while with the lady and her husband, thanked them over and over again for their kindness, and told them we'd let them know if the bird recovered—or really was our Peeper.

Our joy, as we drove home, was mixed with concern for the bird—and uncertainty. After all, other birds got out too. Just two days before, I had seen someone else's beautiful yellow parakeet flying with a flock of sparrows.

For three days, the little bird just slept and ate. He didn't whistle. He didn't say a word—and Peeper had quite a big vocabulary! But on the fourth day, when I got home, Mother had news. 'Our little bird'—and she said it with a happy smile—'came out on his perch to greet me this morning just as he used to. He even nodded and said, "Pretty Peeper; tsk, tsk, tsk; oh dear!" '

Well, we laughed—and cried a little—for joy. Our God is

so big and so great, yet He was still concerned about a little 'sparrow' just as Jesus said. Concerned enough to give him back to us for six more years!

The
Windup Dog

A True Story by Irene Aiken

IT WAS ESTELLE'S eleventh birthday, and she was very happy with all her gifts. 'But I like the windup puppy the best,' she said, rubbing her face in its soft fur and looking over at me. The dog was brown and white and had a mechanism inside that made it spin and wag its tail, nod its head, stick out its pink tongue, and even bark.

It was a gift from me, her cousin. I had spent all the money in my piggy bank on that doggie. I had seen it in town and fell in love with it. Mother said, 'No, it costs too much. You must look for something cheaper to get Estelle.'

'But I want to buy this. It's gorgeous, and Estelle will love it.' I had felt choked because I wanted it so much and I loved Estelle dearly. 'Besides, it's her birthday,' I added, as if that made it all right.

So Mother had let me spend all my money on it, and Estelle loved it, just as I had known she would.

She lived on a farm and I lived in the city, so we couldn't get together as much as we wanted. It was a special treat when we got to stay together overnight at one of our houses. Tonight I would stay over with Estelle, and tomorrow,

Sunday, I'd go to Sunday school and church with her and her family.

After supper, Estelle and I took time off from our play with the toy dog to study our Sunday school lesson. It was about Adam and Eve on the day they ate the forbidden fruit.

Estelle was troubled about the lesson. Since her mother was also her Sunday school teacher, she went to her.

'Mother,' she said, 'why did God make us so that we could sin? Sin makes lots of trouble and sadness. Why didn't God just make us so we would never sin?'

Her mother smiled. 'Well, Dear,' she answered, 'I guess God wanted us to choose freely to love and serve Him. That's why He gave us a free will. Of course that means we can choose to disobey Him too.'

Later, Estelle said to me, 'Well, if God made us so we could do wrong, why does He punish us when we do?'

'It doesn't seem fair,' I agreed. 'He could have made us good, couldn't He?'

'Of course,' Estelle said. 'I think He should have too.'

Just then we heard a lot of noise outside. Poochy, their dog, was running out to the road the way he did when a car turned up their long, winding lane. We all went outside to see who was coming when it was almost dark.

The moon was a thin cup just above the trees of the nearby woods. Below us we could see the car headlights as it circled up to the house. Poochy's barking was excited and constant.

'Stupid dog!' Estelle said. 'One of these days he's gonna get run over.'

'He most certainly is,' I agreed.

It turned out to be a neighbour friend, Mr. Turner. He had come with his violin for a musical evening with my aunt and uncle.

Estelle and I sat on the front steps and listened to the

sweet tunes coming from the open window as my aunt played the piano, my uncle strummed his guitar, and Mr. Turner fiddled on his violin.

We studied the moon and stars and pointed out those we knew and giggled a lot. Poochy lay next to us.

'I really like the toy dog you gave me,' Estelle said. 'I bet it cost an awful lot.'

'Yeah, it's the best toy dog in the world. But it was worth it,' I said. I was glad that I had made her happy.

An hour or so later, the neighbour man went out to his car, and we all stood around the way people do in the country when guests leave. We yelled things like, 'Hurry back, now,' and 'Ya'll come back, you hear?'

Then he started the motor and Poochy ran out again to bark at the car wheels.

'That dog is gonna get killed one of these days,' Mr. Turner called back as he left. Poochy trailed him down the lane, barking after him when he reached the main road.

Then it happened. Another car came very fast down the road, and Poochy went after its wheels.

We had a quick glimpse of the dog in the car headlights and heard him barking his head off. Then we heard a loud thunk! We saw the car swerve wildly, then straighten up, and go on!

We all ran down the lane, and Estelle was crying. 'I told you Poochy was gonna get killed,' she kept saying as we ran. 'I just knew it.'

Poochy lay crumpled beside the road. He was dead—the side of his head, crushed. Estelle went down on her knees, but her father pulled her up and led her away.

Later, when she and I were getting ready for bed, Estelle looked sadly at the toy dog. 'I guess I'll name this one Poochy too. He can't run after cars and get hurt.'

'He has to do what you tell him when you press one of his buttons,' I said idly. 'He has to obey you.'

'But he's not a real dog,' she said sadly. 'He can't do anything if I don't wind him up.'

We sat silent then, both thinking the same thing, it turned out. I said it first. 'Do you think maybe that's why God made us so we could do wrong as well as right?'

'Yes,' she said, sighing, 'if we could do only right, we would be like this mechanical doggie. God doesn't want us to be just windup toys. He wants us to choose to be good—on our own—and to love Him because we want to, not because we have to!'

We heard footsteps, and her mother came into the room. Estelle told her what we had worked out. 'I think we'd rather be like Poochy, Mother, and make mistakes now and then rather than be like a robot.'

'I think you're right,' her mother said, smiling at us.

'And I want Daddy to get us another real live dog soon,' Estelle said, holding the toy dog up. 'This one is nice but it simply isn't real.'

We said our prayers later. 'Thank you, Lord, for making us real live persons,' I prayed, 'not just windup toys. And help us learn to do what's right—even if we *can* do what's wrong.'

'And, God, if there is a dog heaven,' Estelle added quickly, 'please give Poochy a nice warm place to sleep. And tell him not to chase any more cars.'

'Don't be silly!' I said, giggling. 'There aren't any cars in heaven.'

An Arctic Bear

by Gloria A. Truitt

Along the northern Arctic shores,
   This expert swimmer lives.
He's very large compared to all
   His many relatives.
He's often spotted miles from land
   Upon an icy floe
In his white and furry coat
   That blends in with the snow.
Now, many animals enjoy
   The North Pole's frigid air,
But he's the fiercest of them all—
   The growly polar bear!

The Day of the Dust Storm

A Fiction Story by Doris Steinmetz

DEBBIE MIERS finished her breakfast and pushed back her chair. 'May I feed Quacker before Sunday school, Mother?' she asked.

Mrs. Miers smiled. 'Yes, Dear. Go ahead.'

'Just think!' Debbie exclaimed, 'Tomorrow, we'll have eight darling little ducks.'

'Better not count your ducklings before they're hatched,' her mother warned. 'Eight eggs don't always mean eight ducklings.'

'I can hardly wait!' Debbie chattered eagerly. 'Little ducks are so soft and cuddly.'

Debbie got the water and rolled oats. At the door she stopped. 'Have you noticed how the dust is blowing, Mother?' she asked.

Mother frowned. 'Yes, I hope we're not in for another dust storm. With all the spring ploughing done, there's loose earth everywhere. A bad wind now could be serious.'

Debbie made a wry face thinking of the cleaning and dusting. Their home was near Bakersfield, California, where miles of farmland stretched out in all directions. When the crops were growing, it was green and lovely. But at planting time even a light breeze could stir the dust into clouds.

Debbie went out to the hedge. Quacker had made her nest in a sheltered place underneath it. 'Here's your breakfast, Quacker,' Debbie said, setting the food and water down.

Quacker hissed at her. Debbie laughed. 'Quacker,' she said, 'you're getting crabbier every day.' But she knew Quacker was anxious to protect the eggs from harm.

A gust of wind blew in Debbie's face as she hurried back to the house.

Daddy was looking out of the window, frowning. 'Thank the Lord, I haven't planted yet,' he said. 'The wind's getting stronger.'

'We'd better start early for church,' Mother said. 'We'll have to drive slowly. It's hard to see already.'

Daddy didn't work on Sunday. He believed that if he put the Lord first, the Lord would take care of the crop. And He always had, Debbie knew, for hadn't He said, 'Those who honour me I will honour'? (1 Samuel 2:30).

Debbie was glad that her mother and father were such good Christians. But she felt uneasy lately. They'd been telling her that the Lord Jesus had died on the cross to pay for her sins too. She must receive Him as her Saviour.

But Debbie shrugged off her uneasiness. *I have plenty of time*, she thought.

'Come on, Dear. We're ready to go.' Mother looked around. 'I think we have everything closed up tight.'

The sky was filled with a yellow haze of dust as they climbed into the car and started out.

Drifts of dust sifted across the road. Mr. and Mrs. Miers rode in silence, looking thoughtfully at the dark sky.

By the time Sunday school and church were over, the wind was blowing a gale. Swirls of dirt filled the air like thick yellow fog. People's faces were sober as they filed out of church and started home.

The road, with its white line, was completely covered with dirt. Often, as the Mierses drove along, they couldn't see past the bonnet of the car. Though he drove only about five miles an hour, Daddy had to stop frequently and get out to see if he was still on the road. Once, the car stopped, wheels spinning, and Daddy realized they were in a ploughed field.

He got out and carefully groped his way back to the road. When he got back in the car, his face was pale under the streaks of grime. 'We can't be far from home, but I don't know if we can make it,' he said. 'Our wheels are deep in the dirt. Let's have a word of prayer.'

They bowed their heads and prayed for guidance. Soon they were back on the road. Presently, the white arch marking the neighbour's farm loomed ahead. Home wasn't much farther now, but every inch seemed a mile. At last Mother said, 'Thank God. There's the house.'

But as they turned in at the driveway, fear clutched Debbie's heart. Tiles were flying from the roof. Mounds of dirt were piled up as far as they could see, completely covering the lawn.

'The whole farm will have to be levelled again,' Mr. Miers said tensely. 'There's a big job ahead, but I'm glad I hadn't planted yet. That won't have to be done twice.'

As Debbie ran towards the house, she noticed the drifts of dirt piling up against the hedge.

Suddenly she screamed, 'Quacker is under the hedge!' She knew exactly where the nest was. Frantically, she scooped away the dirt with her hands. Her mother stood watching. Soon she uncovered Quacker's head. But it was too late. Quacker had died on her nest, stretching her head up and up. At last it had been covered with the drifting dirt.

'Look,' Debbie sobbed. 'Quacker's dead—and now—we won't have any little ducks, either.'

Mother drew Debbie gently into the house, and wiped her grimy, tearstained face.

'Don't cry, Dear,' she comforted. 'I'm afraid there'll be more serious casualties than Quacker from this storm.'

'Mother, she must have waited too long,' Debbie sobbed.

Mother put her arms around Debbie. 'Dear, sometimes life is like a storm,' Mother said. 'Jesus wants to be our shelter, not only now but for ever. But so many people are like Quacker. They think they have plenty of time. They put off coming to Christ. Finally sin, like the drifting dirt, buries them so deeply that they can't escape. Then they find, too late, that they're lost.'

Debbie hung her head. She knew Mother's words were for her. Tears began to trickle down her cheeks again. She said, 'Mother, I've been hoping that, like Quacker, I was safe in the storm. But now I'm going to make sure. I want Jesus to be my Saviour.'

"THEY'VE GOT TOO ORGANIZED."

The Intruder

A True Story by Jeanne Hill

I KNEW SOMETHING was wrong when I woke up that morning. Mother was hammering and Mother never hammered! Father was a carpenter so *he* did all the hammering. But he was working in the city all that summer and only came home to our new farm at weekends.

Whatever Mother was hammering couldn't wait until the weekend. Something was wrong.

Hurriedly, I ran outside to the hen house. There was Mother on a ladder, nailing something up on the front door.

'What are you doing, Mum?' I called.

'Hello, Jeanne!' Mother came down the ladder. 'If you'll help me a few minutes, I'll make breakfast. I'm nailing up wooden crossbars so we can lock the chicken house doors.'

'Why?'

'The hens had an intruder last night—an unwanted visitor,' she said.

A ripple of fear went up my spine as I helped her move the ladder to the back door.

'If I hadn't heard the hens squawking at daybreak and come running out, we might have lost them. I guess I scared

114

off whatever it was. I just caught a glimpse of his shadow. But he chased my hens so hard he left a whirlwind of feathers in his wake. Just look at this mess!'

Mother opened the hen house door as she spoke. Buff feathers scattered across the floor bore witness to the intruder. So did something else—a strange musty odour. My arms broke out in goosepimples.

'Mother, that awful thing didn't get White Taffeta, did it?' I asked, suddenly worried about my friendly leghorn. She would be an easy hen to carry away. Named for the shine on her creamy white feathers, White Taffeta was the youngest and lightest of the hens—next to the small brown bantam.

'No, the intruder didn't get anything,' Mother said, as she climbed the ladder at the back door. I handed her the nails and she hammered up the wooden lockbar.

Though I was relieved at my pet hen's safety, I still had a bad feeling about the shadowy varmint that had nosed or pawed open the door to get at our chickens.

But now the hens would be safe. Mother dusted her hands, and we went in to breakfast and our morning Bible reading.

The next three evenings, when the chickens had gone to roost, I helped Mother count the feathery bodies perched high up. When the last hen was settled and snoozing, we locked the doors.

Each morning, Mother was up early to unlock the chicken house. The hens roamed the wide yard and garden until nightfall. At dusk, they gladly came to roost inside.

On the fourth evening, White Taffeta was missing. We waited through the growing darkness, but no White Taffeta. With my torch, I searched the roosts of the sleeping hens in hope that the light would settle on my creamy white hen. But finally we had to lock the doors without her.

The next morning, I carried out the pan of feed early, still hoping to see my young hen among the larger ones that rushed to peck the grain I tossed near my feet. White Taffeta always gently took the grain from my hand. But she didn't show up—then or the rest of the day.

Mother wisely kept me busy. She had me gather cucumbers for pickling. I hadn't picked a pailful when I noticed something white blowing nearby.

I called to Mother and, even while we walked towards the blowing feathers, I knew. We found my leghorn's feathers, scattered at a kill.

Mother stooped and gathered the white taffeta feathers in her hand. Dry brown stains stiffened the vanes on two of them. 'Dear, you know the wild varmint was only after food. He had no way of knowing he was killing a pet. Still, I know this is hard for you.'

She touched my arm, but I felt numb. We followed a thin trail of dark stains on the meadow grass until it disappeared into the woods. All the time, I was imagining my lovely warm young hen struggling against some ugly monster with bloody fangs. How I hated that unseen intruder!

I didn't realize how much I hated it until that night as I told Daddy about White Taffeta when he phoned after supper. He promised to bring home wire to fence in the chickens—but not till the next weekend.

'Daddy, if that thing shows up before we get the wire, I'm going to kill him. He murdered my pet!' Hot tears of hate stung my cheeks. Mother put her arm around me, but I shrugged her off.

'I understand how you feel,' Daddy's voice was gentle. 'It's hard not to hate when you've been hurt or wronged. But while you and your mother are reading the Bible tonight, look at Peter's first letter. He says something special about malice, Jeanne.'

That night Mother and I found these words in 1 Peter 2:1: 'Rid yourselves of all malice.' After checking the dictionary, we decided malice was hatred to the point of wanting to harm others. 'But the monster that killed my leghorn isn't an *other*,' I said. 'It's a thing!'

'Jeanne, why don't you talk to God and let Him decide whether your feelings are right.'

After I was in bed, I realized that awful feeling inside was not pleasant. Still, I didn't want to give it up until I'd spent it on the monster.

The next day was Sunday and church. In his sermon, the minister said something that hit home. 'The longer you wait to take a thing to God, the harder it is to tell Him about it.' By then I was so full of hatred towards the intruder that I felt miserable.

Monday morning, Mother got a phone call from our elderly neighbour, Mr. Wright. His wife was sick.

'I guess you'd better start digging the potatoes, Jeanne,' Mother said. 'I'll help as soon as I get back. I won't be long.'

I nodded as I got the potato basket and hoe.

The sun was high as I worked in the far end of the kitchen garden. My basket was nearly full of potatoes when I heard the hens squawking in fright. Why, that monster must be at the chickens in broad daylight!

'Lord,' I said, as I grabbed the hoe and started running, 'that intruder is asking for it. If you don't want me to kill him, show me somehow, please!'

When I reached the yard, I saw only the scared cockerel running for cover and brown feathers from the bantam fluttering in the dust. Again, that strong musky scent was in the air.

Hoe in hand, I ran to the near end of the hen house. There I caught sight of something bright red as it flashed around the far end of the house after the bantam.

Running through the hens' front door and out the back, I stepped right into the path of the chase. The bantam, squawking in terror, with brown wings spread low and spraddled feet churning, half flew between my legs to safety. The monster? His long angular face peered at me from around the corner.

Fear zinged through my ribcage. I raised the hoe high, aiming to strike him down as soon as he moved from behind the building.

But it was no *monster!* My heart almost stopped beating at the shocking beauty of the creature that slipped around the building. The sun lit up his fiery red coat like a Roman candle at a firework display.

The wild fox and I stood there eyeing each other, only a few feet apart. My arm went weak with relief as the Lord

took away my burden of hate, and the hoe hit the ground with a thud.

At the noise, the fox wheeled and ran. He streaked across the yard and into the trees beyond. I stood watching until his flaming coat was out of sight.

Just then Mother came running across the yard. 'I couldn't kill him, Mum,' I was hugging her and crying. 'God let the fox's beauty show me what He wanted.'

'I know, Dear,' Mother said. 'I saw it as I came from the Wright's house.'

'I guess the real intruder was the hatred that came into my heart,' I said, wiping my eyes.

'And grew into the monster of malice,' Mother added. 'But now you know what to do with hate when it shows up again.'

'Ask God to remove it right away!' I declared. 'Mum, I've just thought of something. I'll be helping Dad string wire to keep the fox out on Saturday, so I think I'll go berrying this afternoon.'

'Me too,' Mother said, laughing.

"I'VE GOT TO FIND A BETTER PLACE TO HIDE THE CAR KEYS."

Other books in this series:

The Giant Trunk Mystery—is a mystery Susie Conroy simply has to solve when Cousin Sophy and her daughter Lilybell arrive in town one spring in the late 1800s with the largest trunk ever seen. Whatever can they have in it?

Sarah and the Lost Friendship tells how life on her family's farm in Canada becomes less fun for Sarah when she and Susan begin to quarrel. Even worse, people start to talk about Christians with grudges. Something must be done to make matters right.

The Peanut Butter Hamster is an exciting collection of animal tales that contains true and true to life stories about all kinds of different animals and their antics, showing how wonderfully God provides for all His creatures.

Complete this coupon and take it to your Christian Bookshop, or in case of difficulty, post direct to: Scripture Press, Raans Road, Amersham on the Hill, Bucks, HP6 6JQ.

please send me the following title/s at a cost of £2.25 each

......................................(Qty)........

......................................(Qty)........

......................................(Qty)........

......................................(Qty)........

I enclose a cheque for: ....(post free)

made payable to Scripture Press